A collection of very short stories, many dedicated to those about to

HAVE A VERY BAD DAY

by

Richard Lovrich

A collection of very short stories,
many dedicated to those about to

HAVE A VERY BAD DAY

Copyright © 2021 by Richard Lovrich

Book design by Richard Lovrich

Printed in the United States of America

The Troy Book Makers • Troy, New York
thetroybookmakers.com

ISBN: 978-1-61468-617-0

Chapter One

FOR THE MOST PART, VERY UNFORTUNATE CIRCUMSTANCES

GOOD SHOT

Cousin Phil, one of a pair of identical twins, nonetheless recognized himself with unerring accuracy in the childhood photos his aunt Erica unearthed after Christmas dinner. His brother Earl was the one who was rarely photographed without an air-gun while Phil was the kid with the patch where his left eye used to be.

DIDN'T ADD UP

Charles made the observation today that, when he encountered a grouping of five objects, he initially saw them as two sets — one with three and the other with two objects. Only when he mentally added them together would they make the total of five. Compounding that revelation was this perplexing mystery. How did those severed fingers, no matter the number, end up in his mailbox? And on a Sunday no less, when there was no scheduled mail delivery?

UNBAREABLE

Without the depth to appreciate women close in age to himself Rupert instead fixed his interest upon Tiffany, whose tautness and charms were the unearned dividends of her evident youth. Unfortunately, Tiffany was actually Martha, who's many reparative surgeries had stayed both the hands of time and pull of gravity. Tonight would be their first date. If all went well, it would also be their last, as anyone who sees her unclothed body must die.

TWO HELPFUL

Mr. Hammerman gripped his chest and collapsed to the floor, his head rebounding and making a vaguely softball-against-bat sound. Luckily, among the witnesses to his fall were Marcia and Geoffrey who both declared that they were trained in CPR. Initially they cleared the space around the unfortunate and unresponsive dinner guest, but which-one of them would perform the lifesaving technique? After some time they did decide - upon rock-paper-scissors.

MEDAL FILINGS

Why merely get up from the couch when you can spring off the couch? Why spring off the couch when you can vault off the couch and somersault over the coffee table? Carlos found the last seat in the urgent-care waiting room, where his own bandaged and clearly blood oozing head was joined by a sullen, moaning roomful of slung arms, wrapped ankles and bound rib cages. Overhead, a dusty, somewhat askew screen revealed in flickers the shamed faces of the injured, eyes held downcast from the live Olympic coverage.

PARTING IS

Mildred was sure that Leroy had affirmed he would meet her on Barracuda Point Beach near sunset at 6 p.m. sharp. So far, disappointingly, she had only found one of his legs.

STAND BACK

Albert violently contracted his muscles, defensively jettisoning a tangle of internal organs through his anus in the direction of his shaman Manfred. The unlucky medicine man, now covered in gleaming viscera, had moments before revealed that Albert's power animal was the sea cucumber. Albert had his heart set on a liger.

TODAY'S LESSON

Aiden had overslept again this morning, so in last-straw retribution, Brittany drew a dick on his head with permanent-marker, woke him up and kicked his ass out of the house. To catch the school bus. For his first day of kindergarten.

HANG UPS

With her hand still on the doorknob and her body framed by the aperture, she set her legs wide, implying an extended stay. But Madison could not remember why she had opened the closet door. Hoping to jog her memory, she began scanning and making note of the clothes hangers. A tangle of dry cleaner wires, a tubular plastic affair in sadly faded make-up pink, a few in clear acrylic, shoulders sagging, defeated by the responsibility of supporting permanently out-of-season coats. Lastly, a lone wooden contraption, bereft of a garment. Heavy of make and pitted with age, it was no doubt the pilfered relic of a long ago hotel stay. The hanger sported a substantial hook, its metal blackened by time and generously rusted with – was that blood? And just like that, Madison remembered what she had opened the closet for.

OVERKILL

For her 85th birthday, Clarabelle's industrious son Ludovik gifted her a robot to help with her care. He had re-programmed Zarbot from clandestine military duty, to push the woman's wheelchair, comb her hair, dress her, brush her teeth, spoon feed her and tuck her in at night. The robot carried out its mission without hesitation. Success was tempered however, by Zarbot's method of locomotion, fashioned as it was after the hopping of a kangaroo; its size, that of a standard double door refrigerator, its weight, at two tons and its pair of pincer tipped, three meter long arms and their action, which was limited to rapid, violent jabs.

SHUTTER TO THINK

The mother and her two small children, clothed in thick, crude garments, stood stonily still, shoulder to shoulder, in front of their newly erected home. Father stood some distance away on a flat topped boulder, the perfect vantage point from which to capture the idyllic scene, while they posed silently, awaiting a sign from father that they could move again. They would all wait a very long time, as it would take another five hundred years for the camera to be invented.

DETOUR

Josephine put pen-to-paper, firmly committed to memorializing nothing but the amicable and happy moments of her life. Suddenly peckish, she made her roundabout way to the refrigerator, carefully avoiding a path through the living room, where the bodies of her family lay, as they always had a way of bringing her down.

NO MIRACLE

Teresa, who was considered very gullible, had received a text message from the Blessed Virgin, requesting that she pack her belongings and wait on the roof. Her friends would soon be surprised twice, as unbeknownst to them and soon to be to their displeasure, she possessed both a ladder and a sniper rifle.

PROMPT AND CIRCUMSTANCE

While Diego couldn't necessarily decide if he felt that the first day of his vacation had been a good or bad one, the loss of his right ear to that Bald Eagle was a stinging reminder that, at the very least, it could have turned out differently.

COLD RECEPTION

Seated near the radio, a bit askew in his La-Z-Boy, Cletus helped to bring in Tara's favorite AM-radio country station. Useless from the day they married, her husband was proving to be surprisingly handy since his recent, untimely demise.

MATERNALIA

Celia's heart was warmed when Jesse took her aside to tell her that she was like a mother to him. But he neglected to tell her that he had, in 1975, committed matricide in order to collect a thousand dollars worth of burial insurance. Which he instead spent on lottery tickets, Colt 45 and cigarettes.

ALMOST FALL

There were times when Sheldon's "Thought-He-Hads" and his "Dids" were indistinguishable. This was just such a time, and the passengers on the plane he piloted were, for the moment at least, blissfully oblivious of his dilemma.

NATURE CALLS

Although he couldn't be absolutely certain that the crows were chuckling directly at him per se, Kirk, never one to lose an opportunity to argue, would not leave the clearing until they ceased. At dusk and after hours of argument, the birds dispersed. Yet Kirk's satisfaction at having bettered them would be short-lived, for no sooner had they left, a particularly bitchy herd of deer arrived on the scene.

WILL, WAY

Felicity was having one of those days. Woefully she also had a chemical weapons stockpile.

DEGREE OF DIFFICULTY

Beatrice was a star in the infomercial world, silently playing characters visibly confused by the exaggerated and clumsily melodramatic use of common products. Each extravagant display was accompanied by a voiceover declaring an "Ouch!" an "Oh!" Or "Nooo!". She had made the operation of toothpaste tubes, a knife, scissors, a can opener, hat, bar of soap, and a sock seem nearly impossible. In a twist of fate, while attempting to zip up her cocktail dress, Bea fractured a vertebrae, fatally severing her spinal cord. Ironically, the contortions necessitated by her zipping as well as the histrionic spasms of her final moments, were neither witnessed, professionally voiced, nor recorded for posterity.

LIGHT HOUSEWORK

Grace's Mom had spared the rod. Unfortunately she had also spared the washing machine, iron, refrigerator and oven.

REALITY, TV

Hanna wanted to watch THE IRREDEEMABLE BITCHES OF LODI New Jersey, Nicole had never missed an episode of COOKING NOTHING SPECIAL ALL DAY AND ALL NIGHT LONG and Kyle was dead set on HOPELESSLY STUPID DOUCHEBAGS WITH TONS OF MONEY. He had the remote, Nicole was wielding a chef's knife and Hanna was passing a can of pepper spray from one hand to the other ... If they had planned ahead and had learned how to DVR, the ensuing massacre need not have taken place.

ART SCHOOL

He did initially try to explain. Tried to reason with her long before he resorted to using force. Even then, he had only tried to pry the piece from her hands – to protect her. Buying an abstract painting at Marshalls was, well it wasn't even a painting! They were both a bit bloodied now, but he had at least succeeded in wrestling the offending canvas from her and destroying it by vigorous stomping. Braydon was certain that when the police arrived, they would assist him in pointing out the error of the poor woman's ways.

CLEAN SPEECH

For Sherry it was all about the dishwasher, which only she must load and which, unequivocally, she would categorically refuse to unload when the cycle came to its silent end. She had considered softening her position, but had turned an unmarked corner and could not find the way back. The negotiator, her boss, mother and the High School Principal, not one, despite their turns at the bullhorn, had volunteered to empty the machine, but instead wasted their time with talk of her guns and hostages.

FOUL PLAY

After having searched in vain across the desert's landscape for two days, and now very sunburned, hungry and tired, Kaden found that he was losing patience with this stupid game of hide-and go-seek.

BIG BANG

Dr. Callius crossed the street in lazy zig-zags, to avoid being hit by any neutrinos. He was of course struck, not by a neutrino but by a Chevrolet, made up of decidedly less exotic particles.

PUT ON

As per the rules of laundry night for the roommates, Jaquan loaded the washer and dryer and Ian would fold all of the clothing. To his wonderment, Ian didn't even know that they made loose razor blades anymore and finding a brand new one in his freshly laundered sock only added to the mystery.

BAD FIT

Gabi's problem with Javier and, in fact, his problem, with her problem with Javier was that Gabi did not like the size of his head, claiming that it was "too big". Well, that was something he could not change, and so Javier would soon forget quirky Gabi — as well as their disappointingly disapproving date. As far as Gabi was concerned, well, she would simply move on and continue her search — carrying along with her a roughly head-shaped box.

OVEN FRESH

Hermione lifted her right ass cheek off the faux-leather seat with mechanical precision, careful to compensate by lowering her right shoulder to a sympathetic degree. The fart was going to come out post-haste and it would be far better, she thought, if it escaped seated, instead of whilst heading for the door of the crowded board room, dragging the rancid, accusatorially faithful, viscous effluence behind her. A momentary bodily wince accompanied the release ... What emanated forth, all but completely silently, wasn't a fetid plume at all, but rather the proprietor of a Parisian Boulangerie, who could not even pronounce the word fart properly and who smelled instead of freshly baked baguettes. No matter how pleasant his aroma however, the baker, like the flatulence he replaced, was going to stick around awhile. She pulled off the most convincing, "who brought the French baker?" shrug that she could muster before returning her guilt tinged gaze to the jangle of financials spread before her.

LOW TIDE

The sun was setting and the bleat of the last ferry's horn distracted Cecily, who cleared her hair with a sandy hand to better hear it. There would be no time to waste if she wanted to catch it and get home that evening, so she hastily grabbed and splayed the handles of her beach bag and jammed into it damp towel, flip flops, lotion and her paperback. Cecily raced single-mindedly through the dunes and for the pier beyond, parting the dusk with her sparkly swim suit. So single-mindedly in fact that she forgot her brother Rudyard, who she had buried nearby-her-beach-encampment, up to his chin in the sand ... Sand which grew heavier and cooler with every inch of the approaching tide. Unable to turn his head to look about, he chided his, now on-board the last ferry sister, for playing another of her silent-treatment practical jokes.

REAR VIEW

Abigail Steele turned artfully away from the railing and the majestic view beyond, exposing her trademark profile to the camera, whereupon the director called "cut". This was the cue for her butt double to step up, lean over and peer, in Abigail's stead, out onto the valley below. Overstepping her mark, the stand-in lost her footing and Abigail watched in shock as her dorsal doppelganger tumbled silently to the rocks below – with HER ass.

CLOSE CALL

Fire rapidly engulfed a modest home on Hummingbird Lane, West Knuckliff, in the hours before dawn on Christmas day taking the lives of residents Eugene and Dolores Ketts, both 88, and their son Randy Ketts, 42, former maintenance engineer at the long ago condemned Cherished Dream Fish Cannery. The tragedy also struck Randy's seven children who ranged in age from 16 years to 13 months of age as well as his three pit bulls five iguanas and two Komodo Dragon lizards. Miraculously, Herman's wife Starlette escaped the blaze without harm along with an also unscathed, and unnamed, male friend of the family who had dropped by for a smoke.

MAKE WAY

Milton's prostate, diagnosed as enlarged, had also become quite enraged and no longer content to block only his urine flow. Expressing newfound ambition, it was blocking traffic leading to the Lincoln Tunnel.

SAD TASTE

Shark attacks had been as uncommon as Lupe was unbecoming, so, while momentarily mourned, she was not in-all-truth going to be missed. Be that as it may and much to the townsfolk's chagrin, the shark, now with an appetite for human flesh, turned its gustatorial attention to dining upon more beautiful, more popular bathers.

FORCE MAJEURE

Under the weather, Charmain had visited various medical websites to ascertain the cause of her malaise and the results were mixed. She was either suffering from Dengue Fever, Spongiform Encephalitis, Rickets, Palsy, The Vapors or, heaven forfend, Haunted Colon. Charmain's general practitioner instead diagnosed her as experiencing discomfort as a result of "wiping too hard".

POETIC JUSTICE

Well known for verses with veiled messages and vague meanings, Gabriella had turned a very special, very personal creative corner in crafting her new collection of compositions entitled "Poems About the Bitch Who Pretended That She Loved Carnations and Hockey and Who Wore Lavender Paisley Tights Which Pointed Like Laser Beams Up Her Coochie-Short, Fake-Ass, Gucci Skirt and How That Husband Stealing Cunt Ended Up Getting Stabbed By Someone. Someone Really Nice."

PATIENT ZERO

The mixture of herbs and a little alcohol was generally likely, just as the carnival salesman had said, to be "good for what ails ya". Unfortunately, what ailed Zachary was a deadly, inorganic, self replicating and highly infectious prion disorder that had been released on earth by a malevolently piloted, alien spacecraft.

PROGNOSIS

The operation was over, Shanice was about to wake from the anesthesia and her chance for survival, despite the unforeseen complications, would have to be considered excellent. So you could say that it all went well ... If you were to overlook the fact that she had not OK'd the, admittedly altogether unnecessary procedure and that Darnell, despite his best intentions and evident natural talents, was not a surgeon of any kind.

TYPECAST

Dawn lived in a building filled mostly with those who, like herself, made their livings pretending, very well, to be others. Hunter, her neighbor and exception, per-contra did not earn his keep as a thespian. There are various factors that could have compensated for this deficiency but Hunter possessed not a single one. Neither did he possess the faculties required to discern that the vacancy in her stare was simply not there for him to fill. Hunter's proximity to Dawn, far too often, always without invitation and far too close for comfort, was by simple definition, stalking. As luck would have it, she was rehearsing for her starring role in a film about an unfortunate woman, herself being stalked and so, she tolerated his behavior as it was, in-effect, unpaid coaching. The movie's production was temporarily halted and Hunter was summarily put under arrest where he waited in prison as Dawn decided whether to press charges. Luck was no longer on his side, as her next acting opportunity called for her to portray a widow, mourning her murdered husband by visiting his killer – in jail.

INSTANT KARMA

Dalip just couldn't understand why trouble seemed to follow him wherever he went. He ran, flaming torch in hand, through the darkened fuel depot to find the answer.

THE JOB AHEAD

Marcus had, but for one fraction of a minute, lived an exemplary existence, yet it would take a disproportionately long period of time to mop up the blood and dispose of all of the bodies.

A VOID

There was light on Mars and shadow, as well as surface features an earthling might find familiar, but there was no life ... Unless of course you counted Ronaldo Ernitt who had, through the unlikely process of deep wishing, transported himself there in 1997 to avoid accompanying his girlfriend Maura to a Jack & Jill bridal shower.

GET HER DRIFT

Donna casually pointed with her pinkie, momentarily freed from its dainty cup's handle, out at the yard, its features abbreviated by the recent snow's heavy blanket. "Floyd is out there somewhere, under all that mess". Her girlfriends were not accustomed to any humor at all from Donna and certainly expected none of such a dark nature.

DETAILS, DETAILS

Shoes, glasses, handbag – all flew away as the air drew her arms and legs into mock-crucifixion. Her face rippled giddily and all she could-see through gust-pummeled eyes was the earth, stretched tautly across a curved magnificence, pulling her unavoidably down. The tragic thing was, Mabel had neither parachute, nor the slightest clue how to skydive.

DO THE JERK

Her dance moves had become erratic and her expression vacant. If Clarence didn't know better, he would have thought that Ida was having some kind of, perhaps epileptic, fit. While he thought to investigate further into her condition, he left the party instead as he knew nothing about girls and wasn't about to learn now.

POST MODERN

Rhonda insisted to herself that she wouldn't trade her battered painting of fruit, in its ramshackle frame, for all the real apples and oranges in the world, but, alas there hadn't been any fresh fruit for some months now. Wrapped in precious plastic bags (were there really so many at one time?) the elements had still taken their toll on not only her painting, but on each and every one of her most precious possessions, things meant to be enjoyed indoors, things that without a roof would soon be no more. She already missed so much and had not seen an animal of any kind or a man for some time now and certainly not a gentleman. But if she did, if Rhonda did come across a gentleman, she admitted to herself that she would first consider eating him.

ALWAYS SOMETHING

Without question, today's was the best view Sidney had ever had from an airplane seat. This was all the more astonishing as his seat was positioned in the very center of the center aisle. Even so, the whole "spinning about, losing a wing and fuselage rent-asunder, right in front of him" thing, along with the resulting wind and flying debris, were all undeniably distracting.

BLACK AND WHITE

"As you can see officer, there is no possible way that I could have been at the scene of the crime as you do not even have a clue as to where the presumably unfortunate Mr. Jackson met his demise and, likewise, the weapon, whatever it might have been – the evidence you desperately need – is nowhere to be found! As for my whereabouts at the time of the alleged murder, I was engaged in my regularly scheduled squash game, for which your own Chief of Police Watkins was my unfortunate adversary, his losing to me again today, bringing the total spoils of my winnings to 12 Rob Roys at the Carlyle in whose penthouse you can come to apologize to me, when you get back to your jobs and catch the killer, if indeed there is one. I wouldn't be surprised if Mr. Jackson isn't lounging on his yacht IN THE MONEY right now, purposefully out of touch with everyone and everything and tacking without a care into the dusk tinged horizon drinking his signature dry martini with lemon infused garlic clove." ... Lemule stood before the police, a blacked bowl in his scarred left hand, in his right, a pineapple chunk can, its open circular saw lid painted in haphazard gore. There was far more blood on his arm, torso, neck and face describing the arc with which he had dispatched JJ, who lay in sadly human tatters at his feet. Lab tests would be run to attempt to determine what Lemule had smoked, whether or not the substance had been a factor in his committing this hideous crime and indeed, whether or not something in the waxy residue, might prove to have been a contributing agent in his fantasmic, golden age of cinema erudition.

CHILLING

Anger, shock, fear – among all human facial expressions, that of joy was the most fleeting, the most impermanent, and Dale had yet to capture it, despite a basement freezer full of faces.

THE FAIREST?

The bubbling pink and grey flesh; eyes on tender, violently jerking stalks; hair whose follicles coalesced into stout, moist, rubbery tentacles; a mouth with lips draped loosely over yellowed, cracked tusks, and leathery, forked, prehensile ears — the mirror didn't lie, Antonin had really let himself go.

HE KILLED

With his ready wit, perfect timing and tightrope walker's balance of mockery and self deprecation, Leland seemed perfectly suited for a career in stand up comedy. He was, in practice, an executioner by trade and unlikely to get big laughs from anyone, anytime soon.

ASHES TO ASHES

On September 16th 2019 at nine a.m. Eastern Standard Time, Nelson Pennelwaitz sat up in bed and declared to the world, with his wife Dharma as his only witness, that he was not himself. By noon the same day, it was apparent that he wasn't anyone else either. At approximately four p.m., Dharma broomed up what was left of him into a makeshift dustpan formed from the travel section of the Sunday New York Times and pondered the appropriate fate of his remains. Ever hopeful, she decided upon the recycling bin.

MAKE 'EM LAUGH

His gold plated AK-47 blatted out a jangly good morning against the thin, echo-less sky, but its comforting chatter couldn't mask President Mondone's growing regret. He had often told jokes to Corporal Katega, who would laugh boisterously. Now, with the Corporal's untimely passing, another good listener would have to be found.

GOAD DAY

On Tuesday, the residents of erstwhile quiet Cherry Street, woke to news of their neighbors' Emma and John Smith's brutal killing. The couple was survived by their twins, son Poopypants Mountbatten Wiffleball Smith and daughter, Cankersore Onassis Philately Smith. Police are searching for clues as to any possible motive that might point to a suspect or suspects, guilty of that senseless crime.

PLEASE

It was harvest festival day and the whole village had laughed and taunted Jose when he shared his dreams for a better tomorrow with them. Now they were silent, chastened and all lined up in the dusty square waiting for the antidote Jose was, thus far, reluctant to dispense.

NO RETURN

It would have been a simple matter to return it, but somehow Percy never found the time nor opportunity. He soon borrowed more, amassing a pile of books among which the original, unreturned hardcover was hopelessly lost. Guilt weighed heavily upon him and he was left no option other than to abduct and attempt to wipe clean the memories of the entire library staff.

THE PERFECT END

Aubrie was a born leader and had that way of making everything look so easy. It came as no surprise then, that when she lost her balance while hiking and fell to her death into a ravine, she did so with such élan that her hiking mates followed suit. Each one of eight, in turn attempted, but fell short of replicating, the perfectly executed forward 3 1/2 somersault, 1 twist in the pike position, that Aubrie completed before being dashed into a crumple on the rocks below.

SO DON'T

Not a care in the world, in this world at least. As for the dark place that Cora could enter by tilting her head just-so, well that was another matter entirely.

CAT NIP

Upon learning from its owners of the paltry reward being offered for the safe return of Princess Socks the cat, Davey, hungry from his efforts, ate her on the spot.

CLEANUP IN AISLE ONE

Her husband Alonzo had left her alone in the vegetable department for just a moment and now Estelle stood over a lifeless grocery clerk, her arms curved in a menacing, crab-like sway, blood augmenting her smeared makeup and adding macabre punctuation to the glittery red typography of her "BEST GRANDMA" sweatshirt. Alonzo's statement to the police was simply, "She never did get out much."

PET PEEVE

Toto, the furry little mammal that Mack had purchased at the mall, although irresistibly endearing, did not bear precise resemblance to the sugar gliders he had found on Google. Nor were the increasingly aggressive habits and rapid growth of his new pet consistent with sugar glider behavior. The fact that Toto, now five feet in length and of robust build had Mack cornered in the family room was more curious still and frankly, somewhat worrisome.

MANSPLAIN

"Stupid, silly Mary, you do not even know how to use a pistol and what, pray tell are you doing with that can of gasoline and in our dining room, no less?"

IPSO FACTO

When Wesley finally broke down and asked his brother in law Gus, the stock trader, for advice, Gus told him that it was a dog-eat-dog world and that Wesley should pull himself up by his bootstraps. Wesley thought about that for an evening and in the early morning beat Gus to death with a pair of wellingtons, bereft of straps. He then removed, pan seared and fed Frank's pancreas to his own dog Judas.

POOF

While it would be tempting to call it magic, witness' statements concur. There was but a thin tail of smoke teasing to where Macauley had been standing, one blink of an eye before. How and why Selena, suddenly a widow, had done it would now become a matter, both of scientific speculation and for the police.

ANGERS AWAY

The cruise was interrupted, its meals, activities and engines paused by a boarding by the Dutch Caribbean Coast Guard, for although they had only demanded smiles, maritime law considered the comedy duo of Carver and Holly to be pirates.

PARTY DOWN

The sun had set, the singing had long since stopped and the revelers had gone home to their warm beds. Everyone but Chester of course, for he was still in the town square, shivering, naked and bound to that brightly painted tree.

TOXIC SHOCK

She knew how deathly allergic he was to any type of seafood, yet the speed with which Grover had reacted to Nora's stealthily blended thick shake left her feeling somewhat unsettled.

TOO SOON

Edwin considered it comic relief, but Daisy found that his nude accordion solo, while indulging in public urination play, was lewd, unfunny, unsanitary and considering the otherwise appropriately somber mood of Mrs. Worsteshire's funeral, entirely uncalled for.

THE LAST STRAW

Miriam left her handbag hanging carelessly from the entranceway banister again. On this occasion however, that simple act of laziness had triggered a response no-one could have foreseen, least of all Miriam, who had been really fond of that old horse.

UPS AND DOWNS

Lana was dreaming of sinking in an untethered and rapidly descending bathysphere and meeting a watery demise by drowning at the bottom of the sea. This was ironic, as she had actually fallen asleep inside the gondola of a hot air balloon set hopelessly adrift, and she was instead floating towards an airless, frozen death, high in the upper atmosphere.

UNFAIR

Ichabod sought medical attention for a tick that had aggressively affixed itself to his groin. The creature was increasing in tumescence with each blood-engorging hour, so he sought out medical attention. Rigorous examinations and deliberation by a team of physicians had come to a an alarming decision. They had determined that it would in fact not be Ichabod, though he had been the one to cry out for help, but the life of the tick that should be spared.

MEOW MIX

Initially, the anthropomorphic antics of Pebbles the cat were quite endearing - watching TV, frowning, playing musical instruments, walking on its hind legs – but lately her behavior had changed, her mood now that of increasing ambivalence, bordering on haughtiness. Far more troublesome, and to owner Harvey's chagrin, she had also begun demanding money. A lot of money.

GOOD COP ...

"Don't worry Billy, you can tell me who did it, I would never let them hurt you." "Jump Mrs. Gonzalez, they will catch you." "Flap your arms Mr. Lewis, it will put out the fire" Even as the death toll rose, officer Odelmyer's helpful spree continued unabated.

A SHORT PLAY

"Please tell me there wasn't a baby in there."

HUMBLE PIE

The engine of Gary's dull and dented, 25 year old Volvo had seized and in a weak, auto-dealer driven moment, he succumbed to the charms of a svelte new Japanese sports coupe. Ashamed by his ostentatious purchase, there was nothing to do but run it along a guardrail and scuff it up. Later, he lamented looking stupid and careless and not humble as he had hoped.

OFF LINE

First, there was the page that would not load, then there were posts that had disappeared without provocation and photo galleries with pictures of leaves accompanied by gibberish copy. This morning his profile picture had been replaced with that of a lemur, his marital status had been changed to ambergris and his timeline reached sideways through to alternate dimensions. Facebook had gone very wrong and there was nothing – especially with his now very tiny, furry hands – that Herman could do about it.

UNDER AND OVER

There had to be an explanation – and the only explanation that made sense was that he was now underwater, and what's more, that he could breathe underwater. Well, as was often the case with Zeb, he was again only half right.

HOW ODDS

"I suppose I should clean the toilet even if the world was going to end tomorrow?" The likelihood Brian would EVER clean a toilet was so slim, that the chance the world was going to end tomorrow could now be viewed as a relative certainty. At morning's first light, Brian's wife Hermione stood in their driveway, brandishing her dripping toilet brush at the growing, celestial-blemish of that undeniably imminent asteroid.

DIVINE WIND

Prior to the thunderstorm, Lula had tied everything down for safety and in the morning, save for a few fallen branches, it all still seemed to be in place. Until she checked the seemingly unaffected master bedroom from which her husband Rudy, inexplicably, had been whisked away. The cruel gale had also surgically extracted their new neighbor Ms. Schermerhorn and her Pomeranian Princess Aurora.

APPOINTMENT WITH DESTINY

When the videos of Osama Bin Laden's death were broadcast, they came as a Mother's Day surprise to hair stylist Jeanette Glauberflats of Troy, NY. There on CNN was the man who's beard she had been paid to trim, darken and relax! The high fee, blindfold, the plane and SUV with darkened windows, they all made sense to her now. "He wanted me to do his pubes and I said HELL NO!" They had laughed together while watching Spongebob on VHS over tea.

I THINK I MAY, I THINK I MIGHT

Another evening's observations were at an end, the star flecked sky consumed in the maw of the dome's slowly enveloping, opposing arcs. Anatoli, for fourteen years, lone operator of the Mount Klapper observatory, had spied the heavens through the largest telescope on the West Coast. On this night he wondered, if only just for a moment, why after all of those years he had never considered taking notations of some kind, never attempted to record or report what he had seen?

INQUISITION

Howard slipped and fell in the H&M's dressing room and landed, wearing nothing but Jockey shorts and socks, in a fire-lit, stone walled room, attended by men whose filthy robes and lined faces were marked by soot. In that stuttering, smoke filled dark, one thing was easy to see, that only the devil could account for the strange appearance and meaningless babble of the smooth faced man.

BODY DOUBLE

Manny wasn't the policy holder per-se but rather the person who tracked down, captured, dismembered, ate and then assumed the form and identity of the policy holder. Nevertheless, he nodded affirmatively.

KEPT

Tristan was never ever late for work but on that sunny Monday morning commute, he tempted fate and dared failure by turning left instead of right at a key intersection. This detour lead him to a never-before traversed set of roadways through unfamiliar neighborhoods punctuated by unknown landmarks. As luck would have it, his randomly chosen path proved to be equally efficient, delivering him to work – despite the wrong turn – perfectly on-time. There could be but one reason, he surmised, for this positive result despite his attempt at sabotage. That he had no more free will than a caged chicken and obviously had not the thinnest pretense of independence. Instead, he was likely being kept as a pet by an extraterrestrial super being. Tristan decided then and there to test the limits of his unseen controller by walking out, on-to and casually off-of, the roof of his office tower. Back at his desk now, chastened and chilled, he stole furtive and sidelong glances at his office of non-plussed, clueless co-workers.

PET PROJECT

Merak called out for Spot, who uncurled from a nap, shook out shining fur and bounded through the wet morning grass with little tail wagging. Spot pounced onto Merak's lap, where it forthwith tore free, from rib and spine, Merak's vital organs. Alas, Before the domestication of the dog there came, among other experiments, the attempted domestication of the Cave Bear.

BURIED TREASURE

Phillamena was fascinated, obsessed actually, by the traditions and trappings of foreign nations and their various tribes, sects and peoples. The hypnotically droning didgeridoo of Australia, Finland's wife carrying contests, the spitting traditions of the Masai, Tibetan sky burials, the Betel Nut blackened teeth of Papua New Guinea's women and Kimlaka, a traditional greeting ceremony of the Umturi people, performed with a decorative dagger, a stunning example of which she had just discovered protruding from her own abdomen.

FOLLOWER

Hairpin switchbacks were followed by the narrowing of an increasingly shattered road surface. Hardscrabble shoulder began to overtake the blacktop, now rising into a wall that threatened to tip Grayson's car on its side. He ignited his GPS for the solace that fresh directions might deliver but upon startup it displayed a dolphin, a stick and a magnified granule of pollen. His subsequent stabbings at the screen to choose an alternate route produced images of an ibex, violin and a bicycle's derailleur. Grayson pulled over at the next figment and stepped out, sinking silently upward onto the dimpled surface of an indistinct recollection. If this was any indication as to the efficacy of Gino's short cuts, Jeremy wanted none of them in the future.

CUT SHORT

"Oh my god Norma, I'll get to it tomorrow. You act like it's the end of the ...."

Chapter Two

LOVE, SEX AND OTHER HIGHLY PERSONAL MATTERS

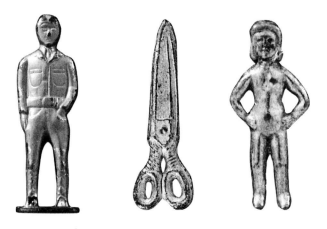

LISTEN CLOSELY

Julius, a leading expert in the field of nano-acoustics, had labored for five years to perfect what, in effect, was the world's smallest and most sensitive microphone and today, for the first time, he would focus it upon a petri dish, with the hope of listening in on bacteria. What he heard, was what every E. coli in town seemed to know already, that his wife Elaine was carrying on an affair with his research assistant Otis.

DAWNING

Vernon flipped the light switch and before the light could extinguish, time, despite the universal law that governs it, paused just long enough for him to realize that Melanie's friend Bernard, with whom she was spending another weekend away, didn't seem at all gay.

COMPATIBLE

Vera had her little secrets from Weston, like allowing water up her nose in the shower which reminded her of being drawn under the surf on the beach-vacations of her youth. Weston of course had his secrets as well, like his having offered terraforming assistance to the advance team of an alien invasion force by identifying targets for their space based laser cannon ships. As all the earth's glaciers would soon be liquefied and the planet engulfed in waves, perhaps their little mysteries were not as incompatible as they might at first have seemed.

FINE PRINT

What was at first a terrible personal tragedy had now become a mystery as well. Lisa had checked all the adverse reactions indicated on all of her doctor prescribed, herbal and homeopathic menopause medications and not one of them listed murdering and dividing up the body of one's husband as a side-effect.

KEEPING THE HOLIDAY

Mr. Elias Grabner regaled fellow barflies with tales of his Lincoln and Washington Days' celebrations of yore. He described each one; the readings from presidential biographies, the raising of tankards of ale and the wanton, commemorative sex acts that he and his partner Amador would fashion to honor each chief executive. Before Elias could finish describing the difference between a

"Toothless Washington" and the "Hole in Lincoln's Head", a nearby listener by the name of Jasper, his sense of nostalgia molested, abandoned his just-delivered Coors Light. He escaped to the safety of his Grand Marquis for a solemn President's Day ride home. Home to the comfort of his bed, his wife Regina and an evening spent perfecting the "Reverse Martha".

HAIR APPARENT

Whilst Googling for male support garments, Carlo had mistakenly come across images of adults engaging in lewd activities. He was shocked to find that neither the men nor women sported any pubic hair, challenging his understanding of human evolution and adaptation. Carlo promptly shaved his body for fear that his primitive condition, through some extremely unlikely series of events, would be exposed. Unlike those who came by their bodily baldness through natural means, he was left with a crimson and irritated groin.

BAD BET

Two days, Four hours, Thirteen minutes. It was a good thing that the casino never closed. But how long could it take, thought

Mona, for a gentleman friend to return from the restroom?

SPLIT DECISION

Louie had half a mind to stop posting details of his personal life on twitter. The other half was busily devoted to posting photos of his genitalia on his neighborhood-watch forum tagged with "missing".

LIP SERVICE

An homage to the wings of Michelangelo's kneeling angel, a brilliant rendition of the ears of Jeff Koon's "Balloon Dog", an allusion to the petals of Georgia Okeefe's "BlueFlower 1918", each creation so very inspired. Today, having crafted his magnum opus, a faithful interpretation of Jackson Pollock's "Convergence", Dr. Pirog, long considered to be the leading physician in the field of vaginoplasty, had without question stretched the limits of his chosen medium.

BAG MAN

Phillip loved Ryan and would've gone to the ends of the earth for him, but not – as it turns out – to unclaimed baggage. While on vacation in France together they had argued about when they would visit, what and who would carry which and where they would eat whatever. They argued so that Phillip had almost flown home, leaving Ryan in Paris. He softened his position though and they returned together, but with Phillip sitting by himself in first class as consolation. That the flight had landed without Ryan's valise was just too bad for him and although later re-routed, it could, as far as Phillip was concerned, sit there at the airport forever, despite – no because – of the fact that Ryan was folded neatly inside.

JUST NUTS

Due to her husband's excessive intake of porn, Felicia felt that there was nothing to do but place parental restrictions on the computer they shared. Graham, now limited to children's programming, became fixated on stuffed licensed characters and soon joined a furry group. He left Felicia for a plump squirrel named Bigtail from Los Angeles for whom he portrayed one Mr. Acorn.

LOFTY

"If you're suggesting for a minute, that I would promote Alain over you, as he can shed his suit, spring gossamer wings from his ample shoulders, lift me off my feet and fly loops around the board room while making sweet aerial love to me, you might just be right." Lloyd should henceforth have been disenchanted of his hopes for advancement, but Eleanor's brutally honest and detailed review, at the very least, gave him something to strive for.

ASTRONOMICAL

Over cereal and the morning paper, Todd informed his spouse Carrie that he had dreamed of her the night before. What he did not share with his wife was that in the dream, he was watching Neal Degrasse Tyson on television. The astrophysicist was using animated graphics to describe the massive distance between Todd and Carrie, which, decreed Neil, would continue to increase for billions and billions of years.

RESTLESS

Irwin collapsed, bloodied and exhausted after successfully accomplishing his latest quest, while Beatrice, seated comfortably and far from sated, began to concoct yet another, impossible trial for him to complete.

DEAD SURE

As unwise as it was to argue given the circumstances, Mae was a stickler when it came to language and simply would not agree to define her cousin Lester's behavior of late as "passive aggressive". Despite the difficulty of making her point while ducking repeated swings of what appeared to be Lester's brand new axe, Mae nonetheless persisted in making her point.

NEW STANDARDS

Antonella had first met Bruno at one of the Eversons' parties and she was quite smitten with him. That was until, when she asked of his interests, he replied "toilet liquor". Fearing yet another disastrous relationship with an ex-convict, she politely exited the conversation, as well as the shindig. Five difficult years later, she ran into him at BJ'S Wholesale Club where they sat and shared a Coke in the ad hoc dining area. In short order and much to her embarrassment Antonella discovered that Bruno was in fact not into "toilet liquor" but that he was actually a "toilet LICKER", they shared quite a laugh and decided to meet again - at BJ's, in deference to his work release restrictions.

THE LESSON

If the love of a good woman was universally desirable wondered Damian, "why should the love of five very good women be so very undesirable"? They were all at the door now and Damian was about to find out.

OLD MOVES

During the village fertility ceremony, Ndele made the ritual mock advances toward Moona, the wife of Beke. Beke in turn responded by performing the customary dance of the jealous husband, during which Ndele, Moona, a family dog and three bystanders accidentally met their fates.

NO GUARANTEE

Let down by his dishwasher's overblown claims of pot-scrubbing ability, Stefon decided to leave Irma, his wife of 45 years. In light of current circumstances, her oft-made declarations of fidelity, love and devotion now seemed far-fetched.

SHALLOW BREATHING

Cassie's love for Chet was ineluctable. His not at all unfavorable feelings for her originated instead from a brittle matrix of conveniences. To forestall his waning interest in her, she had Chet hypnotized into believing that she was the source of his oxygen. While at the mall together, his gaze was drawn by Candy, a languidly traipsing nymphet, who he wandered after, gasping, into the Forever 21.

HOW'S YOUR DAY?

An Andean gale dragged the mottled surgery tent into a starched flag. Inside, a sightless and quadriplegic doctor directed the fine mandibles of an opalescent beetle to attach the nanotubes entering Babette's cranium through the small shaved portion of her scalp, just above her right ear. The other ends terminated in the mantle of a furiously strobing cuttlefish locked in moist embrace with her slender neck. Back home in Cleveland, Babette's husband Taylor pressed the handle down and soon, there would be toast.

MAYBE

Millicent's favorite restaurant, more than a bit too expensive, a table on the patio where she could be serenaded by the gently overlapping breakers, her favorite bottle of champagne served just as she liked it, a bit too chilled and a dozen bluepoint oysters from long Island sound, as gentle as her smile. It was their anniversary and next year, mused Russel, he might bring her along.

CHARMED

"Dear TIME magazine, I was very inspired by your moving interview with Nobel laureate for chemistry Hildegard Klegg. Her story of adversities overcome, challenges met and goals exceeded has encouraged me to work harder, believe in my self and change my life for the better. In lieu of the unlikely fruition of my resolutions, could you please send me a lock of Hildegard's hair, some of her spit, or perhaps a tooth or finger? From any one of these I would fashion or bless a talisman or amulet, in order to afford me metaphysical advantage. Thank you."

REMOTE CHANCE

In the way-too-early winter darkness of the family room, enlivened only by the flatscreen and the flickering, kinetoscopic glow of Family Feud, Heather trained the TV remote upon her quiescent husband Bradley, and with a strained, shaking hand, spiritlessly squeezed random buttons, in the vain hope of effecting some kind of change.

DOORBUSTER

Their anniversary was fast approaching and the freezer that Mike wanted to buy for Celia was on a "too good to pass up" sale, but he still wasn't certain. His concern was that he might not be capable, without unlikely assistance, of lifting her body up and over the edge.

EX ANIMALIA

On his glowing laptop screen, in the fetish section of a popular porn-site, Bill discovered galleries filled with images of himself in lewd performance with his mail carrier Amy, an unfamiliar male sanitation engineer, and an amorous alpaca to whom he appeared to be handcuffed. His dismay was palpable as he had neither memory nor knowledge of any of them or the incidents portrayed. Later, after a cocktail, with further reflection and when the shock of the discovery had worn off, the alpaca did begin to ring a bell.

TMI

"And so, as I have shown, Dr. Slapmeyer had taken my research grants, stolen my lab and my team. I could not sit idly by as he wooed my wife, and in any case, given his much lauded and much plagiarized papers on Ruminal and Postruminal Starch Digestion, my dissolving Dr S. in a vat of bovine bile, was nothing if not fitting." As alarming as Dr. Neider's frank confession to murder was, it was an even more shocking TED Talk.

COOK IN

John, holding the recipe and wearing nothing but a Cognac drenched ascot and boxers, wanted to proceed with caution, while Monique, propane torch in hand and coated head to toe in honey and Rice Krispies, wanted to get on with it already.

THE LOOK OF LOVE

Celine preferred men whose faces betrayed some history, as long as that history didn't include a plague as Zeke's, unfortunately, did. His mannerisms and fashion sense were also corrupt, having originated in a dystopian mirror universe where the gentlemen had, sadly, all been melted down for scrap. She decided to sleep with him anyway as he was her husband and it was their 15th anniversary.

QUICK TURNAROUND

Claudia had always said that she couldn't leave her new husband Paul alone for more than ten minutes. Yesterday, finally, she did, and for a full eleven. Eleven minutes during which Paul had emptied their joint bank account, slept with her best friend Mandi and with her, hit the road in Claudia's own Mustang.

MEMBERS ONLY

Lucinda had no idea that a man could fit his private part in there, no less leave it behind, for her to discover some weeks later.

OUT OF KEY

On the pink stool stood a can of Ensure, positioned just below the keyhole. The can's gaunt bendy straw disappeared through it, into that dark, where instead of drinking from it, Chip wailed resounding apologies against that oaken door. At the same time, Helen, now high over the Pacific, thought that if he were a real man, Chip would certainly have freed himself from that little closet by now.

QUIXOTIC

On her way out of his life, Eve revved her Harley, which unstuck a flock of nearby crows that dispersed and could never be put back the same way again. Sherman examined the empty tree and decided that he would spend the rest of his life trying.

BOTH SIDES NOW

Of the twins, it was said that Shelia could be ambiguous and Ronald ambivalent, but Jerome was ambitious, ambisexual, ambidextrous – and the night? It was still so very young.

OVERQUALIFIED

When he searched online for tips on brain foods, the only result was, "Thou sodden-witted lardass! Thou hast no more brain than I have in mine elbows!" In planning his Italian countryside vacation, Sean searched Travelocity for competitive airline rates, yet the answer wasn't in the form of a price at all, but instead, "whither thou goest you mouldy schmuck, and with whom?!" An on line chat with a lady-friend was summarily interrupted with, "There's no more faith in thee than in a stewed prune, and you are an a-hole by the way". He decided to seek the expertise of his estranged wife Greta, for as a computer analyst with the NSA and amateur Shakespearian scholar, she seemed uniquely qualified to help him get to the bottom of his peculiar on-line privacy problem.

SHE CROAKED

Mylo was filing for divorce from his wife of 32 years, Lena, on the grounds of irreconcilable differences, foremost of which was the fact that she had become a toad. Conflict of personality, difference of interests, resentment and distrust were also listed but were presumed to be the secondary effects of her having been transformed into an amphibian. His lawyer was skeptical and suggested instead that Lena had simply disappeared and that the whole toad thing was a fabrication, or that Mylo had murdered Lena and replaced her, farcically, with a toad. Mylo, after some reflection, agreed that one of those scenarios was likely the truth.

PERSONAL PREFERENCES

With his free hand Charlie tapped in the characters of his personals entry and hit send. – "SWM 32 with gun in mouth seeks the right gal to pull the trigger … Blonde SWF 18-24 petite, but shapely preferred (Jennifer Aniston type). No smokers, drugs, drinking, fatties, skinnies, religious types, hippies, emos, yoga or goth chicks, hangups or baggage".

WELL, READ

Henry was Tina's World Book Encyclopedia – A hulking, anachronistic, pedantic, know-it-all waste of space with nothing whatsoever new to say. For Henry, Tina was a book of self published poems – thin, cheap, unedited, pretentious and far too eager to share its unoriginal insights. That they had found themselves next to one another on life's shelf, gathering dust, was no coincidence.

LOVE IS THE DRUG

Viagra, Cialis, Levitra ... He had tried them all and with no success ... But then again, none of them had actually claimed that they could increase Willie's desire, or even ability, to SPEAK to his wife Bethany.

TO HAVE AND TO HOLD

"Oh Jenny oh Jenny, what was it that drew me to you? What was it that put me under your spell? What was it that has kept me with you here, lo these many years?" And then Lawrence remembered in just that order; The misleading Craigslist ad, the drugged cocktail and the filthy cage in Jenny's basement.

OVER EXPOSURES

Whilst reviewing landscape photos on the Nikon, Francis found his skillfully captured gorges, fens, bluffs and steppes. Curiously, he also discovered unfamiliar images, likely of sun bleached outcroppings. Vexingly, they were distorted, blurry and resembled nothing so much as waggling male genitalia. Flummoxed, he asked his wife Elaine if she had experienced similar problems with the camera when she had recently borrowed it.

PRONE

Elian had lost his first wife Esther in Indonesia to the ravages of the 2004 tsunami. In 2011 near Tuscaloosa, his second wife Marvella met her fate in the hideous swirl of the great tornado. Now with searing lava flow bearing down on the little Hawaiian village of Pahoa, Elian feared for the life of his third wife Trish. He also feared that he might not have enough frequent flyer miles remaining to get her there.

FLIGHT RISK

A pigeon flew in through a family room window, lighted upon the remote, pecked the television to life and then hopped up into the popcorn bowl, where he nestled and fed upon the un-popped kernels. It was challenging, thought Kenneth, seated nearby in the lounger, not to anthropomorphize when you see something like that. That same pigeon subsequently cooed, wooed and flew off with Kenneth's wife Annabelle.

HARD TALK

Lost among the many fine-print warnings on the erectile dysfunction medication's label was this, "The continued use of PRIAPAL may cause lasting, painful erections and may cause the user to spontaneously begin to speak only in Portuguese." On the Newark to Lisbon flight, the mostly male passengers shifted uncomfortably in their seats.

HOMEBODY

Douglas rose to bathe his precious and to brush her hair, daub on her makeup and to wriggle her into her prettiest dress. While the object of his love was less real than realistic, his devotion and dedication to her needs was, in contrast, utterly authentic. How strange it was then, that he began to sense that Diane was losing interest in him, that she was about to leave. He deflated her and left her shoes off for good measure.

ANIMAL TESTING

Dr. Ebersol had come into the possession of a dried plant, unfamiliar to western science, that was used both medicinally and ceremonially by an isolated Amazonian peoples. A plant which, in the unselfish interest of science, she intended to test on herself and her laboratory assistant Hillary, at a nearby motel. Preferably one with free HBO and a hot tub.

NEW RULES

"Listen carefully as choices have changed." Benjamin, used to being rebuffed, was nonetheless thrown by his husband Ric's newest response to a request for sex.

ASSAULT AND BATTERY

Reggie failed unerringly when it came to performing everyday acts, but excelled at those which required daring or heroism. This imbalance led to his wife's attempt to motivate him by placing explosives on the garbage bins, which needed to be dragged from the street, back into the garage by 9 a.m., where a key hanging on a chain could defuse them. Sadly, Mattie had forgotten to motivate Reggie to repair the faulty garage door opener.

WHAT NERVE

Brennan hated the languages and food of other cultures and was unafraid to let anyone know about it. He hoped in fact, to share his point of view with supermodel Helga Loonis and to let her know that he could never tolerate her consuming sushi (or even ordering it) in his presence. Brennan's plan to use a wing suit to fly onto her apartment's terrace from the vantage point of a nearby office tower to deliver his message was thwarted though, by his fears of heights, wing suits, flying, office towers, terraces and supermodels.

SEARCH ENGINE

Searching for a high-back chair, she instead ended up with a low-life boyfriend. In the future, Deidre would have to exercise greater caution when Googling.

WHO WAS?

Their small cabinet of better liquors had matured into closet shelves chockablock with plastic half-gallons of no-name vodka and the gourmet recipes they had prepared together had devolved into a limited selection of pre-battered foodstuffs from portrait boxes that took turns riding the carousel in their sparklingly greasy microwave. When Effie passed away while watching Jeopardy, Sydney did not immediately take note, presuming, for the first few hours, that she was merely stumped.

ONE FOR THE ROAD

Olive was a glass half empty gal and her husband Morris was decidedly glass half full. She had recently begun an affair with Pete, whom she met through friends at work and he didn't even know there WAS a glass.

FAIR WARNING

Handsome and charming, Flora wanted to know why Zane was still single, so she surprised herself and asked him outright. "I guess it's because the other women I have dated weren't lucky". Later, at his apartment and under his cheeky spell, she acquiesced to putting on a silk blindfold. A moment after, Flora felt something pressed to her head and a moment after that, she heard the gun cock.

WHAT MATTERS?

Just what is it that Jacques had seen in HER best friend Luella? What made him cheat and why did SHE go along? Frieda, coolly scientific, had, as a physicist at CERN, access to the Large Hadron Collider and would do the only logical thing. She would drug, and then attempt to propel, Jacques and Luella on opposing trajectories around the 17 mile ring at just under the speed of light, hoping that the resulting collision would throw off particles which might lead to a deeper understanding of their infidelity.

WAS ABOUT TIME

"What in God's name have you done to yourself?" On a brighter note, Charlene's husband Jake had at the very least noticed her new hairdo.

ABANDON

It had taken some time, but in due course, Austin had begun to make love to his neighbor Glynnis, for after all, his wife Judith had left him. To buy groceries as it turns out.

WITH THIS RING

Dr. Maria, her patients all called her that, stretched on a pair of gloves for a routine prostate exam on Mr Ostermann. While probing, she felt an unfamiliar tightness, which upon steady pressure encompassed her index finger evenly. Upon retracting, she found a Claddagh Ring encircling her lubricated digit just above the knuckle. Dr Maria stared cross-eyed at her raised finger, adorned with its curious prize, and at her blushing admirer.

KISMET

The stars were playfully popping in and out of phase, the ocean waves broke with sound of cupped hands being brought together and Clayton was the kind of guy who said hello to everyone he met and who would still open a door for a lady, while Lela was the kind of girl who hid razor blades in her body cavities and didn't take shit from anyone. This was to be their night for love.

BONING UP

Inez had been obsessing upon Internet health sites and was left convinced that walking barefoot would cause pattern baldness in women. Her far more sober husband Rufus chided her, but having done his own web research, discovered that the male organ could become enlarged as a side effect of lengthy rides in elevators. He texted her from the observation tower of the Empire

State Building in hopes that she would meet him there. He asked that she not take the stairs barefooted.

BOY OH BOY

Thus far, in her attempt to net a "bad boy" Essie had only succeeded in attracting a bad smelling boy and then a boy with bad depth perception, who, after misjudging a curb and being hit by a bus, was also now in very bad shape.

PRETTY SURE

Dr. Seligman, filled with consternation while attempting to determine the whereabouts of the peripatetic object of his affection, Judy, had devised the Judy Rosenberg Uncertainty Principle, which states that it is impossible to determine simultaneously, both where Judy might be at any given moment, or where she was about to be on her way to. When he arrived at Narita airport she had already left Japan, having taken a tramp steamer back to Newark.

COLLATERAL DAMAGE

Every man at the Chamberlain High 30th reunion wanted to get into Lorraine's pants, which were tight and already crowded with preternaturally youthful bulges and divots. When she arrived home from the evening's worth of being ogled, she poured herself a glass of Pinot Grigio and began to undress. Mid-disrobement, her Spanx sprang off, striking and killing her only true friend, her cat Mr. Flecks.

OF FEW WORDS

"You had me at – get in the trunk right now or I'll shoot you here."

MODERN LOVE

Irving had a Blackberry, Ida had a Galaxy, he drove a German car, she a Japanese one, he cherished his privacy, she adored sharing the details of her life on Instagram. He liked Springsteen, while she had a growth on the back of her head, the size and consistency of a rotten grapefruit, which implanted thoughts of indiscriminate killing in her brain. It's a wonder how anyone stays together nowadays.

TWO BIT

Bobby Sue and Cooter had gotten to the point in their marriage where they were sick of one another. Well, at least they thought they were sick of one another. The symptoms of their romantic hypochondria continued unabated until Cooter was bitten by a rattle snake – and as luck would have it, Doreen, a herpetologist in fortuitous earshot of his yelp, sucked the poison out. Due to the intimate site of the injury, Doreen and Cooter formed an understandable bond and now, Bobby Sue and Cooter had something real to worry about. Despite of, in fact in great part due to the snake incident and ensuing tryst, Bobby Sue and Cooter, in time, re-kindled their love. They took off for a romantic weekend at Sacandaga Lake. Bobby Sue let Doreen come along just in case, with a rattler.

HEAR NOW

Theresa could be forgiven, due to the clamorous throng at the concert's intermission, for mis-hearing handsome stranger Diesel, thinking he had either said, "I am with the aging Philharmonic but have plans for a special absence" or that "the playing had been bucolic but bland with upended pretense". In either case she found him quite charming and decided to have another, then another drink with him. What Diesel HAD actually confessed was, "I am a raging alcoholic with fast hands and a suspended license" Just post show, and already thoroughly disheveled, Theresa wised up and declined his offer of a ride home.

CONVINCING

Simon thought that his wife Gertrude was very hot, she on the other hand thought that while she had once possessed hotness, had aged out of it . She harped on her lapsed beauty a great deal until one day, Simon, ever dutiful, no longer found her hot either. In time a windfall in the form of an inheritance allowed Gertrude to indulge in her reconstructive re-hotting and it worked, if only for her sake. Simon congratulated this nearly unrecognizable woman on her improvements before moving in with her manicurist Zena.

AUTOEROTIC

Rodney, who worked in IT was, thought Evelyn, nothing more than a harmless flirt. That was until this evening, when, upon leaving headquarters, she discovered him humping her BMW's trunk lid. Still harmless perhaps, but without question, things had progressed beyond flirting.

THEIR SEA

Of all of the waterlogged, barnacle encrusted, pelican pecked carcasses ever to wash up on Sally's beach, Dara's was by far the worst for wear. And yet, and this is the way with an island woman's love, Sally dragged Dara up a dune, far from the menacing crabs and kissed the seaweed from her face. Once inside Sally's home Dara spoke for the first time. In the steely glow, just before daybreak, wrapped in a woolen blanket and crowned with a tiara of fresh snow, Dara was cast adrift, alone in a brine tossed dory, jetsam in the current that took things far away, things never meant to return again.

DIFFERENCE OF OPINION

Wendelin characterized it as a fleeting overreaction on her part, Claude on the other hand, saw it as being shot in the kneecap for his sleeping with Wendy's roommate.

CALL ME

Aput, Kana, piK- pike seer-pok and Lim-uK-suKk. Young Atiqtalik's people had so many words describing snow and yet for her husband OOglu, who was too lazy to shovel any, she could think of only one.

I DECLARE

Pensively buttoned pocket-lids pricked up at the edges and amplified every move of the customs officer's tightly indigo-clad buttocks. A jangle of keys suggestively blossomed from one hip, while a knowingly dented, leather container adorned the other, both slung from her tilting, glossily worn, black belt. She wanted to inspect his luggage, but Larry wanted to inspect her. Before the day was over, one way or another, he expected to find himself in handcuffs.

BARELY THERE

After many weeks of pursuit, there was Catarina altogether nude and standing before Elle, who took her in, inch by goose-bumped inch. Elle smiled and Catarina smiled in shy return. Elle retrieved her notebook and pen from the nightstand while the shy object of her affection bit her lip and blushed, spinning on dainty feet, coquettish, vogueing from one pinup girl pose to another. Elle lowered her head and wrote, under Catarina's carefully penned name and email address "definitely a clothing body". Having satisfied her curiosity, she closed her notebook, rose from the bedside armchair, and in a technical tone said simply, "you can leave now." Catarina grabbed, then brandished the motel room's stick lamp, whipping its cord from the socket. She barred the exit with a shaky but unmistakable warrior's stance, which Elle found to her surprise, quite hot.

TO EACH

Johann described to Emma, in refreshingly few words, the basics of particle physics. Emma informed HIM that she was not wearing any underwear.

TOY LIFT

In 1915, Sir Reginald Smitts would take, on his fated Mount Kilimanjaro expedition, various mechanical devices engineered to, among other things, measure of the earth's mass by determining that of the mountain's. It was while hauling the last of his crates, containing a particularly weighty apparatus to the summit, that he, his guide and two of his trusted bearers fell to their deaths. A century later, melting snows allowed for their bodies to be discovered in a ravine, crushed along with that final crate. It had split open to reveal a machine, operated by coin, which dispensed lewd postcards and vulcanized rubber, adult personal distractions.

SELFIE?

Strike anywhere matches, a can of gas, a once overstuffed, now smoldering chair with its morbid contents and facing it, a tripod with mounted video camera. Hubert's desperate attempt at getting Margot's attention had culminated in today's short lived, and since the camera had not even been set to record, pointless demonstration of love.

EARLY WARNING

Jesús rose early to discover that he was living in an alternate dimension, one in which he wife Maybelline had risen even earlier than he to make him breakfast. He remained in bed, lest he run afoul of other, less fortuitous aberrations.

AND YET SO FAR

"Don't go there" Norman often said. Gigi never got to go there. Still, she dreamed of There, its people, customs, weather, architecture and geography. On the other hand, Norman went There as often as he pleased and Gigi, his lover for four years, had apparently never even gotten a postcard from There.

REAP & SO?

"Let me get this straight. You spend all summer long out there somewhere, doing God knows what, and then this shit happens!?" Jacob's wife Heather, a woman born and raised in the Capital, had many ways which were strange to him, but none stranger than her description of this year's harvest.

ANYONE'S GUESS

"It may be impossible, given current technologies, to count something precisely, as in the number of stars in the firmament or grains of sand in the Sahara, but that doesn't mean of course, that there is a never ending or infinite amount of stars and sand." A sober, scientific and earnest but unsettlingly vague response from Denise, who simply could not give a straight answer to Mason, when asked if she remembered how many lovers she had taken before meeting him.

SNOT HER

In the closet, little used and darker for its contents, Sam rummaged through the cluttered past for his cross-country skis, finding instead, her jacket. He pulled it out as though there were an audience to appreciate his act of melancholy and guiltily began surveying the pockets. They yielded lint, a confetti of pot seeds and pastel wooly balls, a 1989 penny and a used tissue. Ignoring the sensibilities of his non existent viewers, he pulled at the pink Kleenex to reveal a hardness, streaked with grey. With a tearful chuckle he recalled for the thousandth time that Esmée was long gone and her runny nose with her.

ON HIS KNEES

Sterling had never prayed, never considered himself worshipful before that night, but Theda, Theda had a body of biblical proportions.

HIS MOVE

Atticus had decided to lie motionless on the parlor divan for three days in an attempt to deceive his wife Mercedes into thinking that he was dead. Strangely, her daily behavior changed little, despite the apparently alarming circumstances, with the notable exception of course of Mercedes' receiving lengthy nocturnal visits from her co-worker Mortimer, no doubt for consolation.

THE UNMENTIONABLES

While Isla was distracted by a bouncy cosmetics advertisement on the bleary, buzzy laundromat television, Silas concentrated his desires into a beam and directed them upon her soiled laundry. Her attention soon returned to the basket and its singular audience, whereupon the guiltily surprised Silas claimed that his eyes had been drawn to what he believed to be a Portuguese Man O' War, slithering among her unmentionables. Woefully unlikely choice of dangerous animals aside, he felt as though she might sometime soon remember him ... Gravity pulled the weighty and slick jellyfish past puckered Victoria Secret panties and pilly-popped underwire bras alike and there it waited, until later that evening when it absentmindedly, but murderously, stung a laundry basket-emptying Isla. As consciousness dispersed on the way to the bedroom floor, her thoughts were of the stranger Silas who, in regretful, yet insincere hindsight, she wished she had invited home.

CASE CLOSED

"My best friend? You slept with my best friend? WHY?!... Martina did not have to wait long for a reply... "Because you were busy"... Patrick's answer was as simple as it was illuminating and until that very moment, Martina had believed that opportunity and motive were to some degree distinct from one another.

NAY

His left leg at first dragged, then unilaterally pogoed, ultimately hooking its foot on and wrapping itself around a parking meter post. His right hand meanwhile, aided by a betraying arm, flailed and poked at his face and eyes. It seemed as though Jimmy's decision to walk over to Harriet's home and to give her a piece of his mind was hardly a unanimous one.

EXCUSED

In every other way he had been the perfect boyfriend, save for neglecting to purchase a card or chocolates for Valentine's Day. On the other hand, Polly should have taken into account the fact that Windsor, with his shock collar turned up to ten, could hardly have gone out shopping.

SEMANTICS

Emmett put up with Tatum's out-of-control shopping and she put up with his wild behavior, which the authorities, of late, have been referring to as a "murder spree".

THE CHARM

First, a six inch Wonder Woman action figure which he misplaced. Next, a pink unicorn-girl print bed spread which became soiled, torn and threadbare. For his third wife he had chosen a copper colored pigeon he named Aeon Flux and which, during the nuptials, had abruptly flown from her cardboard bridal chamber and out of the nearest window. There was no denying it... Emory just didn't GET women.

A PEEL

Having invented yet another and in his own opinion the best ever, half eaten banana storage device, Oliver reluctantly set his mind on the infinitely more challenging task of keeping his marriage to Clara from spoiling.

ONE AND ONLY

While sporting neither shape, manner, fashion, state of hygiene, disposition, nor outward sign of vitality that most would agree were in any way attractive, Gina's single tooth, which would flash when she was vexed, could hypnotize man or woman as reliably as a movie mystic's swinging watch and with it, bind them in zombific bondage to her desires.

TRADITION

There was a perfect man out there somewhere. Isabella had yet to find him. When she did, she would melt him down with her digestive fluids and assimilate him, as was the way with the women of her kind.

TONIGHT'S SPECIAL

Cody may not have seemed like much of a catch to the other gals, but at the very least, mused Amelia, his ability to sit — with perfect stillness — through tens of hours of porn watching certainly set him apart.

BOUGH WOW

As so many otherwise-innocuous household items could be called into service by Vivian as handy weapons, Jared decided to delay the news of his infidelity until they were outdoors. He had not considered that a sapling, wrenched from the earth by a scorn fueled Vivian, could, with its ragged root ball, suffice as a makeshift, but practicable mace.

AFTER ALL

Walking barefoot and away from a recent incarnation, Millicent stepped on something squishy, which she might have discovered to be Xavier, had she bothered to pause and inspect the source of her momentary discomfort.

TOLERANT

First Katelyn said she wasn't hungry at all and then, not five hours later, she insisted that she was "starving" and wanted to order a pizza. Living with a woman was proving to be far more challenging than Joshua had imagined.

A LOOKER

Eli was alone among Carla's office mates, male or female, in that he never — not once — took the occasion to stare at her tricked up breasts, as they were tautly suspended in the plunging necklines of calculatingly insufficient blouses. Each and every time he greeted her, he did so with shyly downcast eyes, the best technique by far to inspect her feet, which if all went as planned, he would soon have in place of his own.

GOOD TOUCH

Briana accused Owen of onanism, but in his defense, he admitted to really digging playing with himself, but that he was not and never had been, a Viking. Briana found his frankness and cluelessness disarming and only then remembered why she was with him in the first place. The rest of the night went well. She watched.

DO US PART

Olivia's physician Dr. Plottmeyer delicately informed her that the mass of moribund flesh at her side, while worrisome, was in fact her fourth husband Melvin, who she mistakenly remembered divorcing in 2009.

ADDS UP

Trig couldn't count on a third chance with Nina whom he had been two-timing for five months with a Serbian ten pin champion, with whom he had shared a foursome, along with six members of her team, at the Motel 8. Clearly, his days were numbered.

GOING THE DISTANCE

It was Ramone's first Internet incubated date and striding towards the table where

Sylvia was already seated, he saw that – to his delight – she looked as comely in person as in her profile picture. Sad to say, when near enough to extend his hand in greeting, he found that her appearance did not hold up to closer inspection. Three months together now and excuses for being far enough away from Sylvia to find her attractive were wearing thin. In any case, the situation was rendered even more fraught, due to the fact that he was very hard of hearing.

PHENOMENAL

Barry was fully aware that a rock formation of the kind before him might be the result of the gradual force of glacial activity, or from the insistence of swiftly moving water, or perhaps differential weathering. But no, he was going to stick with his first theory, that his ex-girlfriend Jean's new friend Bo had blocked her driveway with those boulders using his shovel loader.

CLOSE EXAMINATION

Gilbert discovered a mote of lint on his laptop's screen, which he mistook for punctuation. He later spied a leaflet for a Chinese restaurant under his windshield wiper, which to his temporary dismay, he mistook for a traffic ticket. Upon arriving home that evening he found a man upon his wife Annette, whom he consulted, mistaking her lover for an ophthalmologist.

THAN NEVER

It was clear now, even from the minuscule, cyclopean vantage point of the well's bottom, that Patsy did indeed have a new hat on.

BEAT IT

"Sixty percent of American women surveyed masturbate twice weekly." Laverne thought this preposterous and furthermore, that Time Magazine was no place for such unnecessarily salacious content. She decided to unleash the resulting umbrage at her husband Egbert, when he returned from one of his vexingly frequent trips to the restroom. Laverne continued to read the already offending article. "One in four men, according to the same study, are masturbating right now."

Chapter Three

LIVES NOT ENTIRELY UNLIKE OUR OWN

NO HURRY

The hotel's dining room was dressed in black for dinner, accessorized with the twinkle of tabletop LED tea-lights. Vincente entered, employing the quietest of be-loafered comportment. Even so, a dutiful waiter materialized before him. "Table for two sir?" ….. "My wife will not be joining me" came Vincente's retort. He hadn't prepared what he would say, but the reply flowed surprisingly easily and said all that needed to be said, at least to a waiter. Of course, he mused, if the waiter had instead been a marine biologist, he might have answered, "No, she will not. My wife was, this very afternoon, attacked and eaten by a large great white shark while snorkeling just off the jetty". Vincente made a mental note just then that he must get around to delivering that very message to the police and even to Ellen's family at his earliest convenience.

OVERDRIVE

Jesus' mind wandered to his bespoke white pearl electric Bentley, with its gleaming bamboo interior trim and simple linen seating. Just yesterday, he and Mohammed, (having left chatty Buddha behind), had taken it out on a freshly paved stretch of highway and at a convent quiet 100mph, they both had what could only be described as a religious experience.

I DREAM

So there Gerard was and there she was and as for getting the genie back in the bottle? He had spent hours trying and so far, he couldn't get her to do anything at all.

HER CALLING

Tangled in a trawler's net, bedraggled, disoriented and despite her scales and fishy tail, she was mistaken for a castaway. Beryl, when sufficiently recovered, decided to stay ashore and ply her trade as a mattress telemarketer, luring men to the depths of pillow-top comfort and order-today values.

HOLE IN ONE

The half peeled potato fled the knife's edge, tumbled across the kitchen counter and bounced wetly to the floor. It continued on its trajectory for the sill marking the border to the dining room, where it sped up for about a tile's length before disappearing. Chanel crouched, knees popping, and reached for the spot where the potato was no more. Her fingertips tingled, then stretched, becoming an elastic tether which drew her in to ... To ask what happened within the kitchen singularity, where time and all natural rules ceased to have any significance would of course be absurd. Suffice it to say, Chanel never found that potato and where she was expelled on, let's call it the other side, it was all potatoes.

UNRIVALED

Mimi's brother Thom, with an H, the wonder boy, was on a rare week away without her. Perhaps while he was gone, she would step up her game and momentarily at least, overshadow him both at home and at school. Thom, free from the binds of everyday family distractions, stood on a sandy hilltop and practiced the levitation of ever larger objects.

DEFINING TRAITS

Eileen was neither all bad nor was she very good, you might say she was just human, a definition not shared with her friend and confidant Cordelia who sported both lungs and gills.

FANTASTIC PARTY

A Centaur clopped lazily-by holding his drink out before him, a swishing censer, anointing the other party-goers with Bourbon as he passed. A Chimera flew in, lighting soundlessly at the buffet table where her lion's head began scarfing up pepperoni slices and goat head reached, on elongated neck and without much success, for the crudités. "This was turning out to be quite the mixer", mused Sherman.

UNDERHANDED

There were no broken dishes, nor was there displaced furniture, ruffled curtains, slamming doors or flashing lamp lights and this was all well and good, but certainly, thought Edna, "a poltergeist should have better things to do than tug repeatably on an unsuspecting persons TAMPON string".

LET IT SNOWED

Snowflakes, big as baby socks, pirouetted around the fenders of plodding, bulbous cars, their tire chains clanking out a familiar tattoo. Kids flapped red plaid penguin arms with glee, their buckled galoshes bearing little glaciers on their toe tops. Gleefully giggling sledders aimed for the billowing phalanx of pipe smoking, fedora topped dads, each supplanting 8 millimeter movie cameras for eyes. Jordan closed the shades and sat, heavily, in his armchair. You see it was snowing outside, but clearly in the wrong decade.

WELL ADJUSTED

After years of failed incantations Sheila had finally summoned Rouland from his bygone era and together they reveled in their shared love of candlelight, sweet wines and harpsichord music. Although in essence 500 years of age Rouland, within only a week's time, had discovered Reggaeton, Legos, Cardi B, TikTok and was like OMFG and ultimately, IDGAF about the simple life.

PIECE OUT

The ever eco-vacationing Smiths had attempted to hire yoga instructors on that sunny Thursday, but instead had cluelessly engaged the services of members of the local rebel forces. When finding the retired pair too insufferable to hold for ransom, the bandits hacked them to pieces which were then strewn about in the brush. Due to the couple's numerous face and butt lifts and various tucks, augmentations and transplants, Celina, a newly appointed Chilean forensics officer, set about looking for seven missing persons ranging from 18 to 75 years in age.

OLD PAINT

Stephie, perturbed by her lagging art sales and cognizant of the fact that equestrian themed paintings, in contrast, seemed to be moving rather briskly, renamed her recent paintings: Naked Martyrdom, My Sex My Death, and Love is Pain, to: Photo Finish, The Home Stretch and They're Off!

QUEST

The cashier asked where, since it had no price tag, Troy had found the item he had ever so gently laid on the motorized belt of the checkout counter. Alas, his search had been such a long one and, exhausted, he could not quickly enough reply. "Is this from housewares sir?" added the azure smocked employee. "Housewares?" Replied Troy bemusedly, "I suppose that is, in the end and given its supreme humbleness, an apt description." The manager soon arrived on the scene, who, after careful examination, added, "was this the last one sir?"... "The last?" Said Troy wistfully, "No young man, this was not the last one, but the only one". This did not appear to be a good answer and the three men stared downward, their silence complimenting the featurelessness that is any WALMART. After a lifetime of searching, Troy was facing his final challenge and with the Holy Grail so tantalizingly close, he could, tragically, feel it slipping again – inexorably – through his fingers.

MY RIDE

While wearing plastic wrist cuffs and being brusquely shepherded by uniformed persons through the phalanx of reporters, Zenia only had this to say of her successful, but now police-shuttered startup "It was just Uber — for vaginas".

VIEW TO A SKILL

More than anything else in the world, Melissa desired a recording contract. If things were not difficult enough in the music business, she had not the slightest talent for singing, nor could she play an instrument of any design. To compound matters, neither did she have the least desire to learn nor practice and her frustration grew with each tunelessly passing day. That was until Melissa woke up, smelled the future roses and recast her goal to that of becoming an ice-road trucker. Surely the acquisition of a trucker's license (despite her dislike of motor conveyances) as well as the mastery of basic reading, could not be as significant a roster of impediments as those imposed by the music industry?

FLY BOY

"Sedentary, subsists mainly on sweetened beverages, communicates only through DM, preoccupied with Pong, avoids sunlight, fancies neither loved ones nor lovers and is perfectly satisfied with a sex life consisting of self abuse fueled by hentai obsession." The black Suburban whisked a bewildered Shawn to NASA headquarters, for the next 50 years of his life and to his entirely unexpected place in history. For you see Shawn had – for the upcoming one-way, solo Mars mission at least – The Right Stuff.

WASTE OF

To Charlemagne, Connor had said, "hey dude" – to Tesla, "what's up dude?" – To Aristotle, "yo dude!" – To Lincoln, "watch out dude". Perhaps the gift of time travel could have been better bestowed.

RESOLUTE

While "scoring more crack next year" was certainly a goal, Valerie suspected that it was not an appropriate New Year's resolution. For one, it lacked any suggestion of a mechanism for acquiring said crack, like getting a job, and also absent were any note of self sacrifice and spirit of self improvement that all worthwhile resolutions should be imbued with. She would have to try again. "I will do less crack next year?" Somehow that just didn't sound right either.

ABOUT TOME

Nothing in the mail again today but bills and unwanted solicitations, nothing. How would one know if their book was being censored? Wouldn't they, whoever THEY are, mail an angry letter, matched to one sent to your publishing house, a letter asking that books be removed from book stores, that all future printings must cease? Or would they send an email, no, that didn't sound right, didn't sound official. Perhaps the first sign would be a letter or, better yet an alarmed call from a librarian – from a brave little rural library, at that – letting Tracy know that her ribald, frank and frankly shocking masterpiece and best-seller had been stripped from the shelves by a local official, cleric or member of the constabulary. Tracy was so filled with umbrage about her book being censored, that she felt motivated to sit down that very day, to sit in front of her computer and finally write the damn thing! But first? She must watch her shows.

DOWN TOWN

Zane had begun to find the presentation boring, so he stepped outside to collect his thoughts. While there, he also collected the thoughts of Dr. Ludovik Kalp, a passerby and astronomer who was at that moment considering the Manhattan Island sized asteroid, silently and inescapably tumbling towards Earth. Zane returned to the meeting with newfound perspective.

SCOTUS

Observing a recent bout of lethargy suffered by his dog Claudius, Gerald telephoned the veterinarian who suggested the visual inspection of the hound's bowl movements for evidence of a probable cause. It took but a moment in the yard, where the dog deposited his poop, to discover the roots of the malady. Claudius had defecated, admittedly poor likenesses, of the current nine seated Supreme Court members on a snowy shelf afforded by a stone planter. The poor quality of the sculptures notwithstanding, the effort required for the dog to create them certainly accounted for his well deserved fatigue.

SPOTLESS

Jason, for whom shower time was a time for ideas, realized while performing today's ablutions that he could not remember washing his body at all from the years 1998 to 2018. He could not even remember seeing the shower, no less setting foot in, or turning on the shower, for that twenty year period. Jason was later relieved to discover that not only showering time, but all of life's recollections from that pair of decades had been cleansed absolutely from his memory.

AFTER SCHOOL

Romy dropped little Jim Jr. at karate, giving his Gi a playful, tightening tug for good luck, then off to lacrosse with Emily, making certain that her socks terminated at the same altitude before mini-vanning cross town to deposit recalcitrant Clara onto the piano bench for her four o'clock lesson — Which left just the right amount of time to squirt through after-work traffic and deliver her little baseball player Max, to his waiting, already bat-swatting instructor … A normal day, but made a bit sad, as Romy had no intention whatsoever of picking any of them up, not ever again.

FAIRY TALE

Sleazy, Raunchy, Easy, Trashy, Tawdry, Lowly and Cheesy, had discovered, on their daily walk in the woods, a sleeping Snow White. They approached her soundlessly, on felt booted little feet and just when they were in stubby-armed, mucky handed reach of her temptingly pink dress, the seven, busybody, do-gooder dwarfs showed up. Just in time, it turned out, to save the day and to avert a scene that would never have become an appropriate children's tale.

FAMILY WAY

In two thousand eleven, learning to set traps for wild boar, Herbie was rent asunder by one of the beasts. In twenty twelve, Philomena met an untimely demise when her overalls became entangled in the shaft of the manure-spreader. More recently, Jeremy was effectively liquefied while trying his hand at bronze smelting. Undeterred by their deaths at six, five and four years of age respectively, the Hendersons, ardent proponents of home schooling, began adoption proceedings for three, new, hopefully far more fortunate children.

ALL CLEAR

Piper's physician had prescribed, in order to bring some measure of relief to her painfully clogged sinus cavities, the use of a neti pot. After a few very awkward attempts which did little more than flood the front of her nightgown, the little vessel evacuated itself successfully into her left nostril. That first flush produced a string of mucus which was followed by a plug of somewhat horny mixed organic material, the sight of which alarmed her. Piper's shock soon surrendered to intrigue, tempting her to fill the pot again and to revisit the same nose-hole. This time what flushed out was, in this order, a fetal mammal of some kind, a single grayish five millimeter fresh water pearl, a Capodimonte

Last Supper ceramic tableau and lastly, an escalation, including the deployment of armored divisions and use of air strikes, of the sectarian conflict in Didjibistan. She considered the potential International implications of subsequent nasal irrigations carefully before treating her right nostril.

TOPLESS

Trudy, a member of the country club for 23 years and frequenter of its swimming pool, had held her tongue about many other violations, but this new bather must be reported for his variations from pool etiquette, safety and hygiene. For his part Jaques had already contemplated leaving, as for one, he was beginning to feel unwelcome and in addition, the sun was beginning to taunt his fully exposed brain.

SIZE MATTERS

Mrs. Timis described one as being "as big around as Napoleon Bonaparte's chief astrologer's gallstone". Mr. Klatterer said "half the diameter of an adult tapir's testicle" and his wife added, "They were approximately the width of a seed from the African Entada Rheedii plant". What at first was a meteorological investigation into the hailstorm of June 2012 in Germantown NY, was quickly becoming the study of a community populated with persons who used extraordinarily obscure units of measurement.

IN COMMON

Jerry of Crossings Falls, Indiana followed Paul, who shared images of his windowless, nondescript home on whose walls hung haphazardly fixed pages covered in indecipherable advertising. Paul, who smoked handmade cigarettes alone and in groups, who pointed while laughing to gaily printed food packaging, who posed with formidable looking male and female friends wearing fatigues in charred villages and who today posted a picture of himself hoisting an assault rifle in his left hand, while blithely kissing a decapitated human head held by its hair in his right. And to think, were it not for Facebook, they might never have become friends.

FINE CHINA

The most clever thing was not that Alexis had mastered Cantonese so perfectly and at such a young age, but that she had gradually but effectively convinced her parents that it had been their own native tongue, a language in which they had become, for unknown reasons, illiterate.

DIG IT

Gone for over two years, Zoe's world wide search for ancient artifacts had actually taken her no further than the local Marshalls' home accessories department. The dogeared letters describing her dig-site encampment to her family had been weathered at and sent from the nearby Sunsetter Trailer Park. Zoe would soon return home to her husband and three children, but she was no more an Archaeologist than was she an agent with the CIA, the agency which would soon call her into extended, undercover service "abroad".

GETTING REAL

Lillian was dismayed that television, founded upon its portrayal of fake-realness, was now nearly exclusively programming shows celebrating real-fakeness. She called her local television network to complain, and became a guest on their non-news broadcast. She was then offered her own reality show about complaining about reality show fakeness, in which – along with a gaggle of new, very fake friends – she grudgingly accepted to star.

ADVANCED

Myra found herself alone with professor Gerber at the college social. He fixed an empty expression upon her and his mouth opened into an out of place grimace. His jaw jerkily ratcheted fully downward and out sprang a tongue which, in coincidence with his eyes, began to spin, flecking her face with foul spittle. She turned on her heels and returned to the party shaken by what she would argue was very inappropriate professor-student, behavior.

AVAST YE

"Tell me again why I shouldn't be feeling like a scapegoat right now?" asked Vasquez just as Captain Blackbeard's saber tip coaxed him from the end of the plank. He never resurfaced after disappearing, bound ankles and wrists, into the bituminous, roiling sea. Which was OK for his shipmates, who never wanted to see him again after his un-pirate-like final words.

REMOTE LEARNED

Bram Stoker had never ventured as far as the Carpathian Mountains and yet was revered for writing about them with dark eloquence in his classic Dracula. Ray Bradbury had created his important Martian Chronicles, without, of course, ever being transported to that faraway planet. So why, thought Carl, all the hullabaloo over his having penned mere prescriptions for Percocet, Klonopin and Vicodin without the formality of having stepped foot in medical school?

SPLIT DECISION

Lourdes found her sister Summer's ways generally reprehensible, but hastened to be harsh towards her, as Summ was also in possession of a nanoscaled temper, the keys to their home, and was, after all was said and done, her conjoined twin.

MOON SHOT

Today upon awakening, Jonas sat up in bed and charted a path that would take him to the 7-11 shop, where he would pick up a quart of ice-cream and rolling papers before returning home to his couch, his bag of seedy pot and then spend the rest of the day streaming Kung Fu movies. A grand plan for an adventurous spirit, yet he had tried many times before and failed.

GLAZED OVER

While recognizing that a detour might undo his efforts, Hector could not help but succumb to temptation. He left his place in the throng, causing noteworthy disturbance, filled with righteous consternation. Why would anyone plan a marathon route that passed a Dunkin' Donut shop situated a scant 300 feet from the starting line?

PRAY TELL

"Does everything about you people have to be so fucking spiritual?" Two days in the field among the Uipeti People and Andrea had discovered the limits, both of her patience and of any interest she might have had in her hastily chosen field of cultural anthropology.

BIT PLAYER

Giant poisonous centipedes were not the most popular tourist souvenir, but Louis had patience, no competition, and while he lamented having scant repeat business, neither did he have a single customer complaint on record.

BUSY BODY

Listening to classical music, petting a dog, a short pony ride, puffing a fine cigar, playing Hacky Sack, engaging in a telephone call with a friend, sipping a glass of cognac and practicing hot yoga – each was supposed to relieve stress, but alas they were not working. Next time, thought Herbert, he would try just one at a time.

THE PUPAL

Dorothy always had a lot on her mind, a lot to say, but was muted by the speed and cleverness of her peers' conversations. Tonight at the coffee shop she leaned into the circle implied by their steaming cups and her lips parted — but nothing at all came out, not one word. Dorothy slipped off her chair, curled up on the floor and pulled out her hair, which she used along with saliva and nearby lint, to create for herself an effective cocoon.

THRONED

King Elwood the First had, in the two weeks since his coronation, knighted, conquered and decreed — but he had not, despite his wife's protestations, attempted to leave the guest toilet.

WORK RELEASE

In a family noted for its underachievers, Boone had distinguished himself as its pre-eminent ne'er-do-work. Susan was looking for a man that wouldn't go astray but in choosing him she had, to her dismay, found a man that couldn't go anywhere at all. Over the course of a month, she moved their computer non-work station, at which he sat while awake, inchingly towards, and then out of, the door of their ground floor apartment. There on the sidewalk, first mistaken as a street vendor and after hundreds of inquiries, Boone began preparing the taxes of passersby.

PASSING FANCY

"Credit or immortality?" Seth looked up from bagging his own groceries. "Excuse me?". "Credit or immortality?" repeated the cashier, her grey eyes framed by what, save from a beneficent smile, would have been a severe face. Fumbling a lime to the floor he asked again, "What did you say?" With a melting scowl she asked again, "Credit or debit?" Seth held his ground in stony silence so that time and opportunity, which had of course moved on, might better find him if they were ever to return.

ALL'S FAIR

Nettie's mother possessed a slithering body and when cornered, struck out with pitiless, scimitar fangs. Her father was gaseous, poisonous and chimeric. Her sister Maddy was odorous, covered in bony plates, and could flatten, when alarmed, to slink under a couch. Her grandfather was a teetering monolith of crumbling concrete who threatened to crush everyone in his path and her aunt Odessa, who held indelible grudges, was comprised of a leathery tube from which darted, without much warning, an ivory spike, Thanksgiving was just around the corner and Nettie thought that she had better gird her loins. Just in case, she would rehearse slipping into an apparently comatose state, thereby distracting any attacker and thusly leaving them open for the kill, dispatched by her sharpened ankle spurs.

FAR AFIELD

Upon winning the Nobel Peace Prize in physics for deftly circumventing the Observer Effect in Particle Physics and Quantum Mechanics, Caleb Joplin stated, "I guess I just sneaks up on-em kinda quiet-like". Notably, his chosen field of study was neither Physics, nor even Chemistry, but "Chickens".

ENEMIES IN-STORE

The recent clashes between the GSCB and DSSG forces had taken on a more violent tone and the city's citizens cowered in their homes hoping the new year would bring a truce. One could be forgiven for failing to remember that those acronyms had meaning long ago and that arming both the Grocery Store Cashiers & Baggers as well as the Department Store Santas & Greeters had once seemed like such a good idea.

MINISTRATION

Patrice lay silent and motionless, his mouth distorted against the tile of the guest bathroom floor, legs woven through wash basin pedestal atop which, threatening the edge, stood the requisite, empty bottle of painkillers. This over-wrought tableau, lit however blandly by the fluorescent dome ceiling fixture, was a ham-handed attempt to distract his wife from his most recent marital misstep and to replace what would, by all rights, be her anger, with sympathy, with pity. The ruse had apparently fooled her, but all too well it seemed, for even as he began to mumble and squirm his way out of faux torpor, he discovered her standing over him with his own shotgun in one arm and a crucifix in the other. She would later tell the jury that this was her own version of off-the-cuff last rites.

DROPPING IN

Yogi was admired among his peers for his extensive and scrupulously catalogued collection of bat guano. His peers were, per contra, neither chiropterologists, coprologists, nor scientists of any stripe, but were instead like himself, professional candy sorters. Which of course begged many other far more troubling questions.

CAUSE AND EFFECT

Lamentably, the rushing torrent had cut a new channel straight through town, resulting in the loss of hundreds of homes and transporting countless villagers to watery graves. Jerome, who through neglect had caused the accident at the dam, was first on the scene — to see if the fish were biting.

POLL DANCE

President for life Barando had fled the country after the blood stained insurrection and his people were, at long last, to have the vote they had fought and died for. In the first round, the people voted to take the right to vote away from the Mela, an ethnic and political minority. In the second round of voting, followed by much public revelry, the people voted unanimously to take the right to vote away from themselves.

HAPPY DAY

While showering, Carlo spied a pair of soap bubbles that had formed on the cap of a shampoo bottle. They floated about and morphed to form a smiley face. Cheered, he later released 60 of his hostages and killed only seven of the remaining 14. Anyone could see that things were beginning to look up .

STRONG WORDS

After Arabella delivered her commencement speech, an absolute silence fell over the Central High School auditorium, paying homage to the steadily deepening blanket of snow outside. She closed the notebook on her hand scrawled poem, CAROUSEL OF SHAME and stepped away from the lectern.

DAY TRIP

Tina made her way through the murk of her living room where, obscured by a taciturn moon, the skulking arm chair pitched her into the depths of an accomplice rug. She fell unabated by weft or warp, floor or earth and woke on a sun blanched beach, head dizzy from the surf and smelling faintly of seaweed. Tina rose, unsure of her balance and with feet confused by a betraying beach towel, fell to the waiting sand – between whose grains she freely slipped. What a day this was turning out to be.

HEAL THYSELF

The residents were either relaxing after a lifetime of very arduous work, or, as she was beginning to suspect, they had never put a great deal of effort into anything and were instead, experts at little-deserved leisure. Sharon was there to care for them, but perhaps it was they who should be advising her, advising everyone, letting everyone know how to celebrate the little things, how to celebrate nothing, so very satisfyingly. She collapsed – a nurse-white and sobbing heap – into a nearby lounger.

HELP FULL

It had come to his family's attention that their Uncle Otto, the former sausage maker and brewer, was still hale and hearty at the age of 92, but at long last in need of a little assistance. Each and every one of them sprang into action to meet his needs. Grandniece Mimi fashioned him an iPad cover using his own blankets to produce the felt. Her sister Penelope did away with his larder of preserved meats and placed him on a strict vegan and gluten free diet. Their cousin Bruce had Otto's daily growler of stout replaced with two droppers full of craft-infused wild elderberry, rose hips and echinacea bitters. His step-granddaughter Clara sold off his furniture and used the proceeds to build him an awesome website and just when the mobile version went live, it was updated with news of the discovery of Otto's chilled, gaunt, withered, but curiously fragrant body.

INTERPRETATION

Klom was a deity of very few words. It is said that he spoke only once, declaring ... "Please be good to one another." His followers became, in due course, a murderous lot.

SCIENCE TIMES

It was while placing a plastic bin of blueberries down and feeling its thin sides buckle under tension, that it dawned on Chanel just what a unified field theory might look like. Moments later, lost in reverie, the lip of the container was caught on the edge of the counter-top sending fruit to scurry across the tiled floor, suggesting to Chanel, all at once, the real shape of the universe. Cleaning up and while reaching for an errant berry under the fridge, the secrets of both dark matter and dark energy were revealed to her. Sitting cross legged on the tiled floor, a bit light headed from her achievements, Chanel wasn't exactly certain what was going on. But she sure as hell wasn't going to leave the kitchen.

NOPE

It could be argued that abandoning the conclave and adopting a social media campaign to choose the new pope wasn't the wisest idea ever contrived. Nevertheless, in the two weeks since assuming his role, Pope SmartyPaws the First had done no harm, save adding a few claw marks to the arm of a seventeenth century divan.

TIN SOLDIERS

In an effort to update traditional customs, challenged by new government and social restrictions and owing to the fact that their ancestral lands were now a sprawling suburb, the male descendants of the tribe attempted to fulfill the requirements of their manhood ceremony by tracking down, spearing, skinning and dividing up a box of Pop-Tarts.

CONCEALED

Confining tailoring, pesky zippers, befuddling buttons, serpentine laces, cloying elastic. Wanda hated all the fuss required by wearing clothing of any description and recently had taken to donning a Hoodie-Footie Snuggle Suit at home and at her state job where she need only add bedroom slippers for propriety. Of late though, this mono-attire became a bother for her as well, so she tried moistening her body with lotion and rolling in lint, which did not adhere evenly. She later attempted a spray application of thinned-down pickup truck bed liner, which coated her body faithfully, but restricted free movement. She eventually instituted a regimen of hormonal treatments, and in six months, was enrobed in satisfyingly thick fur.

GOOD MORNING

"Archie, looking at today's map, all I see is

darkness, there is nothing left for me on this earth." "Time is no longer in motion Boris, we float, aimless atoms, in an eternity of nothingness." Archie and Boris, the friendly morning news anchors had recently gone the "honesty" route during their popular pre-Weather Report banter and today, perhaps they had gone a bit too far.

MISS CARRIAGE

Although she could not remember bringing a single one home, Chastity could no longer ignore her now impassable den with its rush hour traffic jam of hodgepodge baby carriages. Strollers, prams, joggers – some simple, others elaborate. But how and when had she collected so many? A more serious question still, then crossed her mind. What, Chastity wondered, what had she done with all of the babies?

SURPRISE INSIDE

There in the driveway was the gleaming gift that would be remembered by the Smith family, for generations to come, as the Trojan minivan.

NO

Savoring his last bite, Jessie thought to himself that this cheese log at Lori's shindig was the very best he had ever eaten. Was there any reason, really, to go on living in what would most certainly be a world now diminished by this brush with true perfection? Jesse's final decision would put his friends, including Lori in a very awkward position. That of chuckling when reading his suicide note.

IMPASSE

"When faced with an obstruction son, just close your eyes and dive in." This was rare advice from Matt's erstwhile unhelpful father. It is worthy of note that Matt was employed as a filter cleaner at the local waste treatment facility.

AIRTIME

Jarvis dug, spiting imperiled hands, amongst the torn cans, shattered bottles, chicken scraps, various fast food containers and general household jetsam that made up that trailer-side, rustic garbage heap. Neither very new, nor necessarily fangled, his iPhone had nonetheless proven itself to be a surprisingly effective missile in his grandfather's hands.

ONLY CHILD

Although they rarely had visitors anymore, Moe had decided to err on the side of caution and to fish his father's corpse out of the swimming pool and then bury it. Upon reflection, it seemed to him that these tasks most often fell to him. First his mother, then his sisters and brother and now his father, it was really exhausting work and entirely unfair. He nevertheless got to work. For after all, he was the only one left.

SMELL OF SUCCESS

Watching the Olympic balance beam coverage, Mina remembered a different time, when a little Mina, full of hope, stood in a gymnasium before the laser-straight Beam. That daunting device seemed to stretch to the horizon, a horizon beyond which lie personal fulfillment, years of practice and perhaps, just perhaps, Olympic glory. But on that particular day, that particular Beam led straight to an exit door and beyond that, to the cafeteria and the guarantee of cheesy fries.

MAKE A WISH

Despite a typical, quiet workday with nary a personal interaction to note, Edgar still held out hope that somebody, anybody might be planning some kind of surprise for him on this, his otherwise perfectly friendless and well-wish bereft birthday. What he did find, upon arriving home, was that his living room was filled with unfamiliar laughing, naked revelers both eating and smearing one another's bodies with what he preferred to assume was his birthday cake. This carried on for hours during which not a single attendee acknowledged him. By dawn's early light, they stumbled out singly and in friction-red ruddy pairs, all without so much as a single goodbye. While not much of a party from his point of view, it had been, he had to admit, thoroughly surprising.

SHE'S SPECIAL - SO SPECIAL

"Penny's Law" had just been signed, due to the tireless lobbying of her parents, Jean and Clarence. An amazing accomplishment as Penny was neither sick, injured, deceased, nor had she been wronged in any way.

POLL DANCE

Biff Carner's campaign slogan "I'll swing through Washington red tape" had served him well, winning him his party's nomination and thus surprising the pundits, who had all assumed there was little chance at all for such a young candidate, especially one with a prehensile tail.

ON SECOND THOUGHT

"The blue shirt came out really well this time, didn't it Mr. Reynolds?" Brent thought this was as good a time as any and replied, "Mrs. Chin, not a big deal, but my name is Mr. Ryan, Brent Ryan. I thought to correct you before, but it just didn't seem that important". "Oh But – OK Mr. Ryan"... Standing in the door jamb and surveying the parking lot, Brent could not see his car. Looking down he spied hands, shoes and slacks with which he was entirely unfamiliar. After a long and deeply held breath he turned for a moment and added, "Please, never mind what I said Mrs. Chin, Mr. Reynolds will be just fine, yes, Mr. Reynolds".

LAST RIGHTS

As her car descended, it remained remarkably level and so did Rachael's composure. The weightlessness she experienced, which should have induced panic, instead generated a giddy jiggle in her midsection. Vaulting through the bridge's guardrail had momentarily shocked her, but all in all, Rachael was finding the accident fascinating. Dismay did set in, mere feet from the water's inky surface, when she realized that no one would ever know how tastefully she had met her end.

COME TRUE

Belinda lived by one rule and one rule alone, that she would treat others as she herself wished to be treated. Unfortunately for those around her, Belinda's wish was to be treated to vigorous nipple tweaks and prolonged genital caressing.

DEAD OR ALIVE

Gidget, feeling lonely, unloved, ugly and impatient, searched the web for tips on instant beautification. She happened instead upon a post, detailing the method for instant beatification. Later that week, despite having performed no miracle greater than getting out of bed and despite the fact that she was still very much alive, Saint Gidget exited her apartment building and pressed her way through an adoring throng, their faces and hers streaked with joyous and confused tears.

GONE BOY

A wedge of a lime had gone missing and a chilled Corona with it. They were there one minute and gone the next. Doors opened and closed, television channels changed, her minivan pulsed in and out of existence in the driveway and dishes she could not remember using piled up in the kitchen sink. Having an invisible husband, despite the fact that Elena was the one who had rendered him so by ignoring him so absolutely, had become very discomfiting.

GUEST SPOT

Henry tossed and turned through a nightmare in which he had a small penis. In the dream, this condition dismayed his wife Gladys to the point that she left him for his own best friend Chaz. He woke sweatily, only to remember, with no uncertain dismay that he didn't have a small penis but instead a penis that his wife Gladys despised, almost as much as he despised her. To his further dismay, he discovered that, of course, Gladys hadn't left him, but was sleeping soundly next to him. Queer consolation arrived when he noticed that, spooning to her other side was a snoring Chaz, with whom Henry could at least chat during breakfast.

TOMORROW

Glowing, dead squirrels stacked like cord-wood some with Post-it notes on their heads. A charred woman suckling a coelacanth in the shade of an upended oak, roots in the air fruiting bone china in a Delft pattern and cell-phones floating by, ringing and suspended as if in aspic, making their way in a northerly direction. A faraway din, not unlike a jackhammer let loose in a dumpster filled with mink enrobed Coke bottles and the smell of burnt muffler, cinnamon Yankee Candle and pine-apple lollipop. Lebron had apparently slept through what he could only surmise had been some sort of apocalypse.

TIME OF DAY

Louis forgave Vickie her moody and impet-uous mornings, she forgave him his distant and often absent evenings and the life they shared consumed the rest of day. When she found Louis rummaging in their neighbor Claire's skirts and at noon no less, their temporal balance was upset. When night fell, Louis vowed to limit any future indiscretions to his appropriate time slot. Vickie waited till morning, struck him about the face with a waffle and left in an Uber.

COUNTRY CROCK

With Erin engaging in one torrid affair after another to satisfy her sex addiction and Travis' second drug arrest in so many months, the Bronx natives decided to move away from the negative influences and unavoidable triggers of the big city, to far more pastoral environs in upstate New York. The couple adapted to rural living in short order and with surprising alacrity. There they lived renewed, peaceful lives defined by Travis' very successful, single-sourced, organic, fair-trade and artisanal heroin business and Erin's Non-GMO, naturopathic and farm fresh, free-range vagina.

GONE GIRL

The cod, snow leopard and rhino were all but extinct and that should have been warning enough, but Courtney never could take a hint.

MOMENTARY URGE

Naiomi had planned on having a child someday. That plan was to reduce the energy expended, attention required and costs accrued for that child's rearing to that of a cat. Not an exotic and needy purebred, but a tough-as-nails rescue-puss that savored every questionably sourced and wizened pellet of dollar store dried cat food that clinked into its bowl. But first there would need to be the acquisition of sperm, that sounded messy and the rigors of the resulting pregnancy, simply beneath consideration. She supposed that there could be adoption proceedings, the preparations for which seemed very complicated, with too many prying eyes, too much human contact. In the end, Naiomi's need to sacrifice the precious floor space that would be required for the child's litter box was the deal-breaker.

NEXT

After the carboniferous pall that Rocco's last wife Lucia had cast across each and every attempted twinkle of his heart, angelic Diedre, tossing sheaves of golden tresses, donning gay shifts and bounding into his life on lilting gait, had joyously initiated the reconstitution of his desiccated soul. So why then, watching her slumber now, lit by the romanticizing glow of a summer moon, couldn't he help himself from wondering, just what the hell WAS she always smiling about?

UN-CONTAINED

The half-gallon of whole milk came again, this time not in wholesome goodness, but to command Jill to seek revenge.

YOUR TURN

Before sunrise Lars woke to a sharp itch. He pivoted out of the sweaty palm of his cheap motel bed and stood before a streaky full length mirror. On his inner thigh, just under the once elasticized border of his briefs, poked a hairy little growth. By noon it was basketball sized, by the stroke of midnight it equaled his own girth and on its tip smiled a somewhat familiar face, nearly as big as his had been. Before sunrise Ransom woke to a sharp itch.

SOUVENIR

Dick unerringly delivered sticky-from-the-return-trip, salt water taffy from the Cape. Ruth had proudly unwrapped her annually grainy and out-of-date maple sugar candies from Vermont and Cheryl, who could always be counted upon to return from Florida with oranges, did not disappoint this year. That said fruit might have come from the corner grocer, as evidenced by what appeared to be last year's basket, and not hauled all the way up in baggage from her timeshare in the sunshine state, did not matter. When Dashawn returned to work after a week away, placing a brimming bowl on the break-room table, it was a pleasant departure and surprise as he was known neither for his generosity nor gregariousness. He gently removed the cling wrap that had tautly contained the purple-black, glossy fruit inside and retreated silently to his workspace. Janice, an employee recognized more for her kitchen break-room attendance than that of her appearance at meetings or at her own desk, was the first to grab at one of the delights. The intended snack beat her to it, leaping towards and then onto, the side of her head, where, in a flurry of spindly legs and bloody splatter, the creature deposited a clutch of eggs in her ear canal. This unexpected spectacle understandably disrupted the work day and led his workmates to wonder, just where had Dashawn gone on vacation?

A KEEPER

Uma danced through the house, ears deep in 70's Disco tunes, pumped in sonorous waves from her surprisingly still-operable gargantuan silver cassette boombox, its arthritic, creaking wheels accompanying the beats. The arcane music player had been long-forgotten on the top shelf of a rarely-opened cabinet. Hustling about to those club tunes now reminded her of Brent, whom she recalled despised disco and that very boombox. How ironic then, to see him curled, dried up like that, and gathering dust on the shelf just below it.

FOOD FOR THOUGHT

Mel noticed, at the conference meal break, that other participants of relatively advanced years like himself chewed their sandwiches indelicately and without apparent regard for their appearance. Their grotesque mastications were accompanied by alternating episodes of mouth popping, tongue clucking, needless sucking, open mawed chewing, random gasping for air and tooth debris clearing, aided by their roving, grotesquely deft and splotchy tongues. In response, his own self conscious and careful chewing, was wreaking havoc on Mel's cheeks, which suffered dental lacerations due to the unfamiliar jaw-movement patterns. He died of blood loss later that day in his hotel room. The conference attendees were surprised at his passing saying only that he had "looked really good" at lunch.

GET DOWN

Lillili was the rags to riches, international superstar who rose in fame from her humble roots in a war torn ghetto, with her meghit HAPPY GINAPPI, for which the entire listening world was her backup group. Yesterday, it was revealed that the presumed nonsense-lyrics of HAPPY GINAPPI actually described, in the obscure native tongue of her homeland, the dance of success that the brutal counter-revolutionary forces there performed over and upon the bodies of those they had slaughtered. Sales of the song dipped only momentarily.

BRAYED EXPECTATIONS

Maude was searching for the right voice coach, as she had been cast in her first musical film and was being challenged to sing a very complicated, love triangle song. To make things more difficult, she needed to sing while lying on her back. Maude's costars were, at least, dreamy which was important as she was going to be double penetrated in that scene. The director was very ambitious and had at first attempted to fashion his work as the adult musical rendition of television's popular "Three's Company", but he couldn't get the rights, likely because of the donkey scene. Maude wasn't too keen on that detail either, noting, "I mean, donkeys can't sing, right?".

TOP JOB

Luke's master's degree had not prepared him for the fast paced and cutthroat world of pizza delivery.

NOTHING SPECIAL

It was March 17, Saint Patrick's Day and Marilyn groggily woke to televised warnings of planned, numerous and randomly placed police checkpoints, meant to trap drunken, holiday motorists. How fair was this stepped-up surveillance really, she asked herself, to folks who like herself drank and drove every day of the year?

THIN PREMISE

Unhappy with her body and after many attempts at weight loss, Carny decided to stop eating meat. In short order she began re-posting self righteous, militant vegan,

Meat is Murder memes. She became so angry, filled with umbrage and subsequently hungry, that she ordered Jellied Panda Face from Amazon Prime. Upon taking delivery, she was arrested, deported and imprisoned in a far flung region of China. As her captors served only gruel, she became vegan again, thereby shedding 49 pounds and now, chained to a rock in the open sun, she also looked very hot.

RECOVERY

Though the drug in question was no longer in vogue, Charity had just discovered its pleasures and was quickly hooked. Embarrassed by her uncool habit, she admitted instead to sex addiction, despite the fact that she hadn't had a lover in over eight months. She hoped to address her substance issue in rehab as a mere side-note.

UNIBRO

Unilateral, unitard, unitarian, unisex, unicycle, unibrow, universe! Dr. Fedelesson had labored for decades and now the Unified Field Theory, physics' elusive "theory of everything" was laid bare through the good offices of a simple bottle of tequila!

WET DREAM

At the Guinness World Record Awards Ceremony, Eleanor Pistlethwait had loudly objected to the awarding of a prize, to one Moe Cletes, for his claiming to be "The Only Person To Have Peed While Showering." Later, after actually reading the proclamation, she discovered that Moe had won for "The Only Person Never To Have Peed While Showering." She apologized for the interruption, adding for good measure that she herself had indeed, peed while showering. In any case, Eleanor also took an award home, as it was determined after an interview and beyond a shadow of a doubt, that she was "The Only Hard Of Hearing Person Never To Have Peed On Someone Else While Showering."

AFFLICTIONAL

Esther had not been able to write anything that anyone wanted to read, let alone buy for a very long time, so, in desperation, she spent her last 150 dollars a on a writing class for professionals. After turning in her first assignment, the instructor told her that he loved her work and that, in fact, she should be teaching his class. − Esther stabbed him in the face with her pencil and has many great story ideas now, in jail, awaiting her trial date. So, you could say, it all kinda worked out.

LAST WORD

Someone had been murdered at the evening's fundraising event and Pamela was beginning to suspect that it was she.

HAVE A VERY BAD DAY

ACKNOWLEDGMENTS

Although it is questionable at best, to assume that anyone would desire to be associated with this, the initial publishing of my regrettable tales, I shall thank them nonetheless, as misery loves company.

I must first thank Michael Eck and John Seltenreich for their abiding friendship and ill advised support. I shall also thank Paul Grondahl for his brilliant if misspent encouragement and Paul Rapp for his madcap yet solid brand of legal advice. Let me not forget the ever faithful, Teddy Foster, Darlene Myers, Zeb Schmidt, Brendan

Tenan, Corey Aldrich, Persephone Pomme, Sophia Seletnreich, Tess Collins, Jason Pierce, Jamel Mosely, DJ Trumastr, DJ Nate Da Great and Alana Sparrow, who were all careless enough to be there when I needed them.

How can I thank my editor Peter Delocis? Forever, which isn't a "how" of course, as much as a "how-long". And very special thanks to Ryder Cooley and the Dustbowl Faeries, for the soundtrack to my carnival soul.

Penultimately, I thank my wife and partner Lynne Signore Lovrich for her support, for acting as ready source of inspiration and for being the only person, still living, who knows which of my stories is auto-biographical,

With my last breath, I thank the Alpha-1 foundation, without whom, my life would certainly have been a shorter story.

THANK YOU DEAR READER